DEATH AT THE DINNER PARTY

ELLIE ALEXANDER

Storm
PUBLISHING

To request permissions, contact the publisher at rights@stormpublishing.co

Ebook ISBN: 978-1-80508-061-9
Paperback ISBN: 978-1-80508-238-5

Cover design: Dawn Adams
Cover images: Dawn Adams

Published by Storm Publishing.
For further information, visit:
www.stormpublishing.co

ALSO BY ELLIE ALEXANDER

The Body in the Bookstore

A Murder at the Movies

A Holiday Homicide

This book is dedicated to the women who came before me and sparked my love of mysteries—my mom, Mary, and my grandmother, Lois. You live on in everything I write.

ONE

The rustic wrought-iron chandeliers flickered as the wind howled, rattling the thin windows and sending a cold chill through the room like an angry ghost about to unleash its rage.

"We cannot lose power tonight, Annie," Pri wailed, staring at the tin ceiling as if she expected it to cave in at any minute. She twisted her ponytail around her finger. I recognized her telltale sign of nerves. "The guests are arriving in less than an hour. What are we going to do if it goes out?"

"Candles," I replied, motioning to the tapered candles on the table. "Lots and lots of candles. Didn't Penny say she found a stash in the basement? And if you think about it, you can't get more on the nose than a murder by candlelight. This looks like a movie set. Guests will love it even more if we do end up losing light. We'll roll with it—they'll probably think it's part of the staging."

"Yeah. True. I suppose a murder mystery dinner in the dark does have a certain appeal." She tore her gaze away from the chandeliers and returned to arranging maroon napkins on the long, intimidating table draped in gauzy black fabric. "It's just that we've worked so hard on the menu, the drinks, the food, the actors, the staging, and the timing. I didn't anticipate the storm of the century would happen to hit tonight."

"It will be fine," I assured her. Priya Kapoor (Pri to me) and I had been friends for almost a decade. I could count on one hand the few times I'd ever seen her this frazzled. I wanted her to enjoy the party. She'd been my steadfast supporter through so many ups and downs. Now it was my turn to make sure she got out of her head so she could relax and relish in an evening of murderous fun. "Don't sweat it. We're nearly done with the setup. The food is prepped, the bar is stocked, and the actors are warming up in the living room. Let's make sure to light every possible candle we can find, and, if the power does go out, we'll play it up like it's part of the effect. Our guests have paid for an immersive experience. If anything, it will make the evening all the more *draaa—maaaatic*." I stretched out the word, hoping to make her laugh.

"You're right. Thanks for being my hype girl, Annie. You know how much this event means to me." She chuckled. The dim lighting made her brown eyes glow like amber. Pri, my dear friend and partner in crime, was tall with long dark hair, a heart-shaped face, and a smile that could light up any room—with or without electricity. Our newest venture had been her idea.

Pri worked as a barista at Cryptic Coffee in our small town, Redwood Grove. Our little village was off the beaten path in Northern California, where the coastline merged with the redwoods. Pri's coffee artistry was the stuff of legend. Her unique ability to blend roasts with dark molasses and nutmeg with bright notes of citrusy pomegranate made Cryptic a destination and must-stop for anyone venturing through the area. Pri's fan base included locals and strangers just passing through. One special stranger had recently captured Pri's heart. She had developed a long-running crush on a customer who she had nicknamed "Double Americano" because the mystery woman would breeze in and out of town before Pri ever had a chance to learn her name. Thanks to a fortuitous meeting in the summer, not only had Pri finally put a name to her crush, but they had connected, hit it off instantly, and had been dating ever since.

Even better, Penny Shurr, Pri's now girlfriend, had decided to move to the area and purchased the Wentworth farm (where we were currently awaiting the arrival of fifty dinner guests) for a song a few months ago. I surveyed the dining room, appraising our work. I was especially proud of the mysterious touches I'd added to the mantel—a stack of vintage crime novels with ornate covers, small decorative skulls, two portraits that would hopefully have guests feeling like they were being watched, and an assortment of poison bottles and apothecary jars. The sideboard buffet cabinet was similarly adorned with onyx-and-maroon wine goblets, wine bottles, and a creepy assortment of plastic spiders and bugs.

Not bad for a barista and a bookseller. Okay, well, technically, I was responsible for much more than just selling books at the Secret Bookcase. Working at the Agatha Christie–inspired shop was pretty much a dream, and Hal Christie, my boss, and the owner, had given me complete autonomy when it came to creating events and activities to draw new readers into the store.

Tonight was a special occasion, and I was happy to be able to use my event-planning skills to help Pri and Penny. Plus, it was fun to play up on the Wentworth family history, which was the stuff of legend around Redwood Grove. The rambling farmhouse, orchard, and vineyard had sat empty since the early 1970s. Local residents believed that the Wentworths, one of the original families to settle in Redwood Grove, and anything associated with them were cursed ever since the estate burned down in a mysterious fire in the late 1800s. Their rumored fortune, including rare precious gems and gold, and the entire family had vanished after the fire. The estate had been rebuilt and now served as a historical museum, but the farmhouse had been in deep disrepair for decades. One of the Wentworth cousins supposedly was the last known resident, but they, too, vanished, leaving behind debts and leaving the property in probate and legal disputes for years.

When Penny started renovations, she anticipated tearing out the dated shag carpets and wood paneling, updating the mustard yellow appliances, and getting the electrical and plumbing up to code, but she had greatly underestimated the amount of work the rest of the property required. The orchard, vineyard, barn, and farming equipment needed serious upgrading, which required cash—a lot of cash. She ran through her savings in record time. The good news was that the farmhouse renovations were nearly complete. The bad news was that she was out of funds to continue to improve and modernize the grounds.

That's where Pri and I came in. One soggy October afternoon, I wandered to Cryptic for a London Fog latte to find Pri and Penny poring over loan documents. Things were bleak. So bleak that Penny admitted that if she couldn't raise some capital soon, she might have to sell off and sacrifice the acreage to salvage the house. She had already taken out a second mortgage. Her goal had been to return the farm to its original glory and make it fully functional and profitable again, but that was looking less and less likely, until Pri looped me into the conversation.

"Annie, we have to do something. Work your mystery magic." Pri wriggled her fingers at me like she was hoping I could summon a spell. "You've successfully hosted a Mystery Fest and a film premiere. We need a fundraiser for the farm. I told Penny we'll donate a portion of coffee sales, but that won't cut it." She sliced a loaf of chocolate chip pumpkin bread with a serrated bread knife.

My cheeks warmed with her praise. I'd surprised myself with how much I enjoyed constructing bookish events for the store. I guess it was a bit like unraveling a mystery—building the framework, composing a picture and vision, and then weaving the details together with a shimmery thread.

Watching her cut through the spicy, sweet bread gave me an idea. "What if we host a mystery dinner at the farm? You could do coffee drinks and pastries. We could see if Liam or one of the other restaurants in town would cater it. Then we could hire actors from the community theater to be part of the dinner. I'm imagining a full banquet. One long, shared table—cocktails, appetizers, dinner, dessert. A morose yet cheesy atmosphere. Think of the movie *Clue*. I could write a short mystery. The actors would be seated with the other guests, who would be none the wiser that a murder is about to occur. At some point during the first or second course, one of them would die, fictionally speaking, of course, and then the guests would have the rest of the night to figure out whodunit."

Pri stabbed the knife into the bread and applauded, turning to Penny. "I told you she was brilliant. That's genius, Annie. Absolute genius. And it's the perfect time of year for a murderous dinner. We could host it the weekend before Halloween, hopefully on a dark and stormy night. This is definitely giving me all of the *Clue* vibes. I love it, and I love you." She blew kisses at me from across the espresso bar.

Penny's smile was more subdued. She complemented Pri beautifully. She tended to wear neutral linens and subdued color palettes, whereas Pri dressed in bright, bold hues—deep rust, vermillion, and marigold. She loved layering chunky necklaces and was always sporting a hand-designed temporary tattoo. Penny's personality was a bit more composed and measured. She communicated with sensitivity and exuded an inner calm. "I agree. It's a lovely idea, and it would be a great way to get the community out to the property to see the transformation. The house and farm are such an important piece of Redwood Grove's history and potentially an asset for the future, but I'm afraid I don't have a budget for an event like this."

I understood her hesitation. "You wouldn't need to front any money. This would be a fundraiser to keep the farm operational. We'd need the farmhouse, obviously, but I was thinking that we would set the ticket price to cover the cost of food and the actors, which honestly shouldn't be outrageous. I know Ophelia Timmons, who runs the Redwood Curtain Players, the local theater group; I'm sure she'd be thrilled to give her actors an opportunity to showcase their talents, especially if I write the script."

As the concept took hold, my brain began to spin. I couldn't believe I had tossed Liam Donovan's name out. He owned the Stag Head, a pub in the center of the village square. He and I notoriously had not seen eye to eye much, but lately, we'd begun to form a tentative friendship. His food was undeniably delicious, and I had a feeling that if I asked, he might be willing to cater at cost.

I knew he felt like he owed me after an incident during the screening of a Hitchcock-style film this past summer. I had been attacked, and, for some reason, he had decided that he was at fault for not protecting me. He wasn't. The killer was, but that didn't change the fact that he had gone out of his way to try and do favors for me ever since. At least once a week, a special treat for Professor Plum, my cat, or a batch of house-made scones would show up on my front porch. I had begged him to stop trying to make amends for something entirely out of his control thus far, to no avail. Maybe Penny's dinner party could feed two birds with one scone, so to speak.

"Do you really think we could pull it off?" Penny asked with a newfound touch of hope.

Pri looked at me and reached over to bump her fist into mine. "Have you met this dynamic duo? Hells yeah. I'm all in.

Liam and I can pair up on food and drink. I'm imagining a bloody panna cotta eyeball dessert with fresh raspberry sauce. Annie, if you can coordinate the entertainment, I'll take on the menu. Do you think Hal and Fletcher will help?"

"Absolutely," I replied with confidence. A mystery dinner party was right up Hal's alley. The same was true for Fletcher Hughes, my coworker. I knew without a doubt they would both be thrilled to help with anything we needed.

"How many tickets can we sell?" Pri pulled out her phone and started making notes. "Do you think we could seat fifty in the dining room? It's a fairly big space. We could put tables together so dinner is served family style."

Penny's pale skin flushed with delight. "I think fifty is manageable. What would we charge?"

"We'll have to do some math and work backward after we know the hard costs for food and paying the actors," I said, internally already making calculations. This was where I thrived. My brain was a sponge for a spreadsheet. There was something so satisfying about meticulously arranging and categorizing data.

Pri bobbed her head with enthusiasm as the idea took hold. "This should be high-end. It's a fully immersive dinner theater where the guests are part of the show. I want you to net at least ten thousand, so we'll set the ticket price based on that. Plus, we can do an auction or paddle raise as part of it."

"That would be a nice start, for sure," Penny replied with a hesitant smile. "As long as you're sure. It sounds like so much fun, but I don't want either of you to go to extra trouble. I know you both have full-time jobs and other responsibilities." Penny motioned for Pri to stop marking the date on her phone. "I really appreciate your enthusiasm and willingness to jump in, but this feels like too much."

"It's already decided. We're doing it. We just need to

confirm the weekend." Pri checked the calendar on her phone. "Does three weeks give us enough time?"

"It will be tight but doable," I said. "I'm going to need to start writing a script now." The thought of creating a cast of potential suspects, red herrings, and plot twists made my body hum with eager energy. It could have also been Pri's highly caffeinated coffee, but I'd devoured every mystery novel I could get my hands on from the time I could read. Mysteries had been my escape and outlet for as long as I could remember, but I'd never tried to write one. This would be a fun challenge.

Pri tapped her screen and held it for us to see. "It's done. The date is set. We'll sell tickets here. I'll start advertising as soon as we confirm with Liam and the Redwood Curtain Players. I'm calling it now: Tickets are going to sell out on day one. Everyone in town is obsessed with the Wentworth fortune. Did you know that the Chamber of Commerce is considering putting together a treasure map for tourists? They did a survey, and it's something like a quarter of visitors report choosing Redwood Grove for their vacation spot because of the Wentworth history and the long-lost treasure. I guarantee that people are going to flip out at the chance to see the inside of the Wentworth farmhouse!"

"Really? Are you sure?" Penny winced like it was painful to admit that she wanted or needed our help.

Pri put her phone away and gave Penny a dismissive wave. "This is what we do, right, Annie? It's the Redwood Grove way. We support each other. You said it yourself: The Wentworth farm is a huge piece of our history, and I know many people in town who will want to do anything they can to help you preserve that piece of our past. Your vision of re-opening the farm and vineyard for school groups and community events is exactly what we need. This is more than your personal project; it benefits all of us."

Penny fanned her face, trying to fight back tears. "I don't know what to say."

"Don't say anything—we have planning to do," Pri shot back with a wink. "We're going to need to figure out how many plates and silverware, glasses, tablecloths, and chairs you need."

"And décor," I added. "We want to set the tone for a night of murder and mayhem—a touch of Edgar Allan Poe maybe. You can't go wrong with a raven or blackbird and gothic candles."

"Okay, let's do it." Penny beamed. "This is going to be so much fun. Thank you both. I don't know what I would do without you."

"Can you believe that we actually made this happen in three weeks?" Pri's voice brought me back into the moment. The lights flickered again. "Don't tell Penny, but there have been more than a couple of times when I thought maybe we were in way over our heads."

"You mean we're not right now?" I motioned to the massive table set for fifty. Gold-rimmed plates, maroon napkins, wine goblets, black candelabras, and antique gold vases filled with moody fall floral arrangements with burgundy dahlias, sprigs of blackberries, smoke bush, and hellebores made the dining room feel like a movie set. "Aren't we soon seating fifty prominent guests with hurricane-strength winds raging outside?" I teased.

"How dare you." Pri pretended to glare at me. "You just had me convinced that the weather was *atmospheric*, adding a dramatic flair to the evening's festivities."

"Ba-ha-ha. It is going to be a dreadfully dark and stormy dinner." I deepened my voice and mimicked the *Scream* face, clasping my hands on my cheeks and letting my jaw go slack.

She tossed a napkin at me.

"No, seriously, all kidding aside, I think we're in good

shape." I picked up one of the name cards. Fletcher had hand-written each one with a blood-red calligraphy pen and finished them with a blood-red wax skull stamp. "What's the deal with Curtis Wright? He doesn't want to be seated next to Patrick Zimmerman?"

"Oh my God. Yes. Make sure those two are far, far away from one another." Pri refolded the napkin. "They have serious beef."

"Why? What's their issue? I heard you and Penny talking earlier about Curtis making an offer on the farm."

"He's the worst." She smoothed the napkin and set it next to a gold-rim plate. "He won't take no for an answer. Once he learned that Penny was running out of cash, he swept in like a vulture and made her a lowball offer that, if you ask me, was downright insulting. I think because he's retired and *a man*, he assumes he can get away with treating her like she has no business sense. He's so dismissive and condescending. I'm not a fan."

"That's annoying." I lit a match and held it to the first candle. "He owns the farm down the road. It's fairly rundown, isn't it?"

"Yeah. It's in worse shape than this place was when Penny bought it." Pri repositioned a place setting on the opposite side of the table. "It doesn't say a lot for him, given that Penny has owned the farm for less than three months and has already made tremendous improvements. He wants to get into the wine business. At least, that's the rumor I've heard. I don't think he cares about the orchard. He just wants her grapevines. But if you ask me, it's an odd move for someone who's basically retired. The vineyard needs loads of work, hence the fundraiser tonight. I don't get it—why would Curtis want to take on a project of this magnitude at his age?"

I peered out of the original paned windows as a crack of

lightning lit up the dark sky. "It does seem like an odd shift at his age. How old is he?"

"He's in his mid-seventies for sure. Maybe even pushing eighty. I don't think either of his kids wants to take his place over. They both left Redwood Grove years ago and never looked back, and yet he's hell-bent on getting Penny's grapes."

"Is she considering selling off any part of the acreage?"

"I think her exact words were, 'over my dead body.'" Pri stuck out her tongue and made a face. "She's not going to let him bully her into selling. At least not yet. She has to give this a fighting chance before she starts to consider breaking up her acreage into parcels."

"Good. I'm glad that she's standing her ground." I'd never met Curtis, but his name came up around town. He was notorious for being crotchety with shop and restaurant owners and a lousy tipper. "What's the deal with him and Patrick?"

Pri stoked the fire. If the power went out, we'd still have heat. The farmhouse boasted a large brick fireplace with a mantel in the center of the dining room. I loved the aroma of the woodsmoke and the ambiance of the dancing orange flames, which sent waves of warmth through the room. Handwoven rugs softened the wood floor as thunder rumbled above us, shaking the house like one of California's signature small earthquakes. "That's another story. I'm nervous about those two even being in the same room. According to Penny, Patrick is a developer. He approached Curtis with a very generous offer. He wants to raze the house and orchard and turn the land into a new subdivision. Supposedly, he thinks he can fit upwards of forty houses on the property."

"Has he approached Penny, too?" Like everywhere in California, housing was at a premium. I wasn't surprised that a developer had taken an interest in the farmland for potential future housing. It would be a shame to see the rural spaces around the village disappear.

"Yeah, except apparently, Curtis's property is flatter and has better drainage. He made her a super lowball offer, claiming that the way her grapevines are sloped isn't as appealing—or you could interpret that as financially lucrative—which is fine by Penny because she doesn't want to sell to Patrick either."

"Good." I let out a little sigh as I moved farther down the table to light the next set of candles. "Okay, so note to self: Keep Patrick and Curtis away from each other tonight."

"As far away as possible," Pri said, motioning to each end of the table. "Like opposite sides of the room."

Penny swept in carrying a platter of dinner rolls formed in the shape of skulls. She wore a shimmery sapphire-blue jewel-toned flapper dress with a matching beaded headband. Her hair fell in soft curls at her shoulders, and her lips were dusted with a touch of glitter. "Did I hear you talking about Curtis? Could we just not say his name tonight? That would be fine by me."

"Hold up. Where's my girlfriend with a closet full of beige?" Pri's eyes sparkled like Penny's party dress at the sight of her. She swept over to kiss Penny. "You look amazing. Am I dating a supermodel?" She turned to me. "I don't know about you, Annie, but I'm feeling very underdressed. I need to change soon."

"Me too." I blew out the match and tossed it in the fireplace. "Penny, you look lovely."

"Thanks." Penny set the bread in the center of the table, her hands trembling ever so slightly. "What were you saying about Curtis?"

She seemed as jittery as the fringe on her skirt. Usually, she had an air of quiet calm about her.

"I was filling Annie in on him and Patrick," Pri answered, brushing her hands on her jeans. We both brought outfits to change into after we were done with setup.

"I'm about this far away from throttling the man." Penny smooshed her thumb and index finger together. "He's outside causing a scene with Patrick right now. The only reason he bought a ticket tonight was to try to intimidate me. He wants the dinner to bomb. It's another way to try to bully me into selling. I have news for him: None of his intimidation tactics are going to work."

"Don't worry, we've got your back." Pri moved closer to Penny and reached for her hand.

Penny forced a smile. "Thanks. I appreciate it and everything you've both done. I'm sorry to be such a downer. This far exceeds my expectations." She paused and placed her hand over her heart as she took in the dining room. "It sucks that Curtis is such a beast, but honestly it's not just Patrick who needs to be kept away from him tonight. I need a big glass of wine and zero interaction with him. I don't trust myself right now. I'm literally trembling because I'm so upset." She held out her hand to show us. "If he says one more thing to me, I might snap."

"We'll play defense for you," I offered, hoping to reassure her. I knew how much pressure she had put on herself and how much was riding on tonight. "You can simply enjoy yourself and impress all of our guests with your grand visions for what the property could become with their generous support."

She nodded in agreement, but her smile didn't reach her eyes.

I felt more determined than ever to make the dinner a smashing success. Pri had been right—tickets sold out within a day of posting about the mystery dinner, and in addition to the proceeds from the meal, we intended to cap off dessert with a live auction. Instead of gift baskets, we had arranged experiences. Fletcher offered to take a group on a haunted walking tour of Redwood Grove, Pri would host a mystery coffee tasting and latte art class at Cryptic, and one lucky winner would get to have the Secret Bookcase all to themselves for an after-hours tea party. Penny agreed to open up the farmhouse for an overnight stay, complete with ghost stories around the bonfire and s'mores. The giveaways were unique and compelling, in my humble opinion, which hopefully would encourage guests to be generous in their donations.

A loud thud sounded in the living room, followed by shouting.

"Great." Penny exhaled and shook her head. "I have a sinking feeling this is exactly how tonight's going to go. I've been a wreck for the last hour because I can't shake the worry that something bad is about to happen."

TWO

Pri, Penny, and I hurried in the direction of the commotion. The rambling three-story farmhouse was built in the late 1800s when the Wentworth family first arrived in Redwood Grove. I couldn't imagine how isolating and remote life on the farmhouse must have been in those days. Even now, with modern technology and basic electricity and plumbing, it still felt like stepping back in time. Each room in the house felt like it had its own story to tell. Hardwood floors, worn smooth over the years, ran through the formal dining room, living room, and now converted office. Wainscotting painted a soft cream lined the lower half of the hallway. Penny had torn out the carpets and old wallpaper, refurbished the floors, and updated the entire main floor with different modern wallpapers that still kept the tone and aesthetic of the original house.

I felt acutely underdressed in my dusty jeans and hoodie as I stepped into the living room. I brushed off my hands and scooted against the fall wall, huddling next to Pri.

The room was a long rectangle with an ornate stone fireplace as the central focal point. Penny's redesign retained the original feel of the house. She had installed a modern botanical peacock wallpaper in elegant shades of navy with pops of yellow and gold. A three-piece sofa set in lighter shades of complementary blues was arranged in front of the fireplace. The actors participating in the dinner were gathered around the fireplace, reviewing their scripts.

A little thrill came over me when I realized that those were my lines and words they were about to read tonight.

An older gentleman with a shock of white hair that stood on his head like the peacock feathers on the wallpaper pattern leaned against the carved mantel, snarling at everyone. His skin had seen plenty of sun. His grizzled frown and intimidating presence made it impossible to ignore him.

"I'm guessing that's Curtis," I whispered to Pri.

"The one and only. I told you he was impossible to miss." She rolled her eyes.

"I've asked you nicely to leave, Curtis. Twice. I'm not asking this time. I'm telling you to get out." A woman wearing an eggplant-purple flowy cape and black combat boots twisted her ringed finger with a flourish as she pointed to the entryway. "I cannot have my actors distracted before a performance. We have an entire process we need to go through—visualization, vocal warm-ups, humming, lip trills, character work, and quiet before we go on stage. This isn't a typical show. This is improv. My cast has a few key points and lines to hit, but otherwise, they will be engaging *in character* with the dinner guests on the fly. Do you understand the level of concentration required for this kind of performance?"

"Improv, got it. Isn't that acting for hippies? What do you have to practice if you're making it up as you go?" Curtis shrugged nonchalantly and picked up a ceramic vase. He blew imaginary dust from the vase and planted his gaze on a young actor sitting on the edge of the couch. "I'm not leaving until I have a word with Jeff."

Jeff chewed on the collar of his white chef's coat. He had

been cast to play the chef role in the mystery I had written. It was a basic plot involving four actors plus Ophelia, the director. To have the mystery flow seamlessly with the meal, the hook was that Jeff, aka the chef, would work in the kitchen with Liam, our real chef. When the actor playing the role of the victim drops dead after the soup course, Jeff becomes the top suspect, and it's up to the guests to work together to solve the crime and apprehend the killer before dessert is finished.

"I cannot let that happen," Ophelia, the director, responded, holding one arm out to keep Jeff seated. "Jeff is our key player and is in the middle of rehearsals. You're not supposed to be in here anyway, Curtis."

Jeff hid half of his face with his chef's coat like he was hoping to disappear.

Curtis's bushy eyebrows reminded me of two aging caterpillars. He narrowed them in a hard slant at Jeff as if daring him to meet his steely gaze.

Penny jumped in. "Curtis, Ophelia is right. You're not supposed to be inside. How did you get inside anyway? Guests are queuing up outside. Go join them." She pointed behind her. "The doors don't open for another thirty minutes." Her tone was firm, but she fiddled with her long strands of fake pearls as she spoke.

Curtis held the vase up to the fire. For a minute, I thought he was about to toss it into the crackling flames, but he put it back where it belonged and moved toward the entryway with slow, measured steps, keeping his eye on Jeff the entire time. "We're not finished. Is that understood, young man?"

Jeff kept his head down, intentionally avoiding making eye contact with Curtis. He continued to gnaw on his coat like he was hungry and needed a snack to tide him over until dinner was served. It was good that he wasn't preparing any food because I was sure chewing on your uniform wasn't up to code in a professional kitchen.

Penny followed Curtis, I assumed, to make sure that he actually left to wait with the other guests.

Ophelia clapped twice to get her actors' attention. "Listen, people. I'm not a fan of that man. However, his interaction is a good example of exactly what you will be up against. Distractions are going to be part of the game tonight. Remember, you must stay in character at all times, no matter what happens and what guests might throw your way. Understood?"

Everyone nodded.

She paused and caught my eye. "We have quite a special guest amongst us—the playwright is here with us this evening. What a special occasion. This is your opportunity to ask her any last-minute questions or clarification you might need on your character's motivation."

I felt my cheeks begin to burn with heat. Playwright was a stretch. I had sketched a rough plot with a few twists and a touch of humor, but it was hardly a complete script or worthy of being staged.

"I'm going to run and change," Pri excused herself, keeping her eye on Penny. I could tell she was worried about her girlfriend, and understandably so.

"Go ahead," Ophelia encouraged, making small circles with both hands. Her cape floated around her, giving her an ethereal, otherworldly aura. "Now, my players, what do you need to know to get deep into your character's psyche? This is your opportunity to ask our playwright for any clarification you may need to fully embody your roles."

No one responded.

I wanted to slink away with Pri. I needed to change as well, and I wanted to check in on the kitchen and make sure that Liam was good to go with the first course, but Ophelia kept looping me into the conversation. The truth was that there wasn't much more I could offer in terms of character development. I hadn't gone that deep. The script was meant to be used as a guide or blueprint with a few key plot points and twists. The rest was up to them.

Ophelia scowled and cleared her throat. "My fellow Redwood Curtain Players, let's see some life force. Where is the energy? You are about to go on stage, metaphorically speaking. Tonight, your stage has no barriers. No one is off-limits. Every guest is part of our inclusive production, and I expect nothing less than extraordinary performances from each and every one of you." She inhaled deeply, closed her eyes, and then opened them slowly. She rocked her hips from one side to the other and then focused her eyes on me. "Annie, what would you like to add?"

I was taken off guard. I hadn't prepared a speech or even planned to speak with the cast. "Uh, I'm sure you'll do a beautiful job with your roles. I'm excited to be a part of it and can't wait to see if any of our guests will be clever enough to figure out which one of you is the killer."

She motioned for me to continue. "And what is your expectation of our troupe as the playwright of this esteemed material?"

I was at a loss for words. This wasn't Carnegie Hall or the Globe Theatre. "The most important thing I can say is for you to have fun. Guests are expecting an immersive mystery experience and I know they're eager to put their sleuthing skills to the test."

Ophelia's lips thinned as she frowned. She was obviously disappointed in me, but I had nothing more to add.

She turned to her actors. "Remember, you're getting paid tonight. You can officially call yourselves working actors. Let's stand up. Let's move our bodies. Let's embrace our roles." Her arms drifted to her sides in rhythm, like a butterfly emerging from its chrysalis.

I appreciated that she was trying to energize her actors and that she was approaching the direction of tonight's performance with the utmost professionalism. But I also wanted to remind her that, ultimately, this dinner was meant to be fun and campy. If the actors were over the top, that was fine by me. In fact, it was better. We hired the Redwood Curtain Players for that reason and also because the community theater members were volunteers. They acted for the love of the craft. The Redwood Curtain Players was a non-profit organization. Everything from set construction to costume design was driven by volunteers. That meant we could offer them a small stipend for tonight's performance as a bonus for Ophelia and her acting troupe. It was a win-win for all of us.

I watched as the actors followed Ophelia's directions, standing and rolling their shoulders back like they were preparing for a yoga class. I laced my fingers together and glanced toward the dining room. Could I sneak out now? It was nice to get to meet them, but I had plenty to do before we opened the doors shortly.

"What if someone guesses who the killer is before we've hit all of the points on the script?" one of the actors asked, looking at me. His tan trench coat, fedora, and pocket notebook gave him away as the detective.

I started to respond, but Ophelia cut me off. She was sending mixed messages. First she was practically hounding her actors to ask me questions, but when they did, she jumped in.

"Misdirection, remember? Shift suspicion. That's your entire job. When in doubt, call out Jeff. Make him join the table and begin questioning him about his food preparation techniques. Or point to an unsuspecting, innocent guest. Get everyone involved. You're the detective. Take the lead. Remember, you have a creative license tonight. Use it. Embrace it. Embody it."

I decided that was my cue to take my leave. Ophelia had things under control. There was nothing new for me to add. "I can't wait to see how it all comes together," I said, rubbing my hands in anticipation. "Break a leg."

I wasn't sure if that applied in improv, so I gave them a quick wave and headed for the stairwell before I got dragged back into a conversation about character motivation. The creaking staircase that led to the second floor had been refurbished with a fresh coat of paint, a thin stair runner, and a collection of framed black-and-white photographs of the farmhouse and orchards in its heyday. I paused to admire a picture of the Gothic revival house with its white clapboard exterior, dormer windows with black shutters, steeply pitched gable roof, and wraparound porch.

Penny had done a remarkable job of maintaining the aesthetic of the 1800s architecture while making her new home functional and cozy. Upstairs, there were a series of bedrooms, each with its own view of the vineyard, and two shared bathrooms. My bag was in one of the guestrooms with east-facing windows that provided a glimpse of the sprawling orchard. Rain lashed against the window and pounded on the roof with such force I thought it might cave in.

I unpacked my dress. Since tonight was festive, we encouraged everyone to come in cocktail attire or something inspired by the Golden Age mysteries. I had opted for a velvet emerald green wrap dress to enhance my green eyes and red hair. The dress wasn't like my usual bookstore attire—a T-shirt, skirt, and cardigan. It was embroidered with striking golden snakes on the pillowy sleeves, a plunging neckline, and a slit up one side. I paired it with dangling snake earrings and sheer black tights.

I stood back to appraise myself in the mirror, adding a touch of shimmery lip gloss and bronzing blush to give my skin a subtle glow. I tucked the left side of my hair back with an antique gold barrette.

Not bad, Annie.

I could almost pass for a character spending the weekend at a grand English estate with Hercule Poirot.

I felt good about my outfit, but I couldn't dismiss the flicker of anxiety that rumbled through my stomach. Maybe it was because of the storm or Curtis, but a nagging worry filled my mind that something might go terribly wrong.

Before heading downstairs, I took a minute to inhale through my nose, hold my breath, and then release it slowly. The technique helped center me.

You've got this. It's going to be great.

Tonight is for Pri and Penny.

You've prepared. You've written a witty and twisty script. This is your element and your time to shine.

My pep talk and intentional breathing did the trick. I gave myself one final glance and went downstairs to the kitchen, guided by the ambrosial aromas of sautéing onions and garlic.

The kitchen was attached to the formal dining room through a wide door. Like the rest of the house, it had been tenderly updated with polished wood floors, slab marble countertops, new cupboards, and an oversized farm-style sink. A large island in the center of the room provided extra workspace. Copper pots and pans hung from an iron rack above the island. Herbs in sweet terra cotta pots bloomed on the windowsill, and vintage cookbooks and old canning equipment served as décor.

Liam Donovan had his back to me when I entered the room. The steamy windows dripped with condensation. Soup bubbled on the stove. Plates of mini quiches and crimson beet carpaccio waited at the ready on the island.

"How's it going in here?" I asked, resisting the urge to swipe one of the thinly sliced beets drizzled with a balsamic reduction and sprinkled with goat cheese. The carpaccio was Pri's idea for a bloody yet elegant starter.

Liam wiped his hands on his black apron. He let out a low

whistle when he turned around. "Annie, you look, uh... incredible."

I gulped and hoped my tendency to turn as bright red as the beets when I was nervous wouldn't betray me. "Thanks."

"That dress is smoking hot." He brushed a strand of hair from his eye but didn't adjust his gaze. Liam was ruggedly handsome with a hint of stubble on his cheeks, well-defined muscles, a confident stance, and just the right touch of charisma.

My skin suddenly felt like it was on fire.

Keep it together, Annie.

I tried not to focus on the way Liam's wavy dark hair fell over his eye. Or how his sleeves of tattoos flexed as he lifted a heavy pot on the stove.

Liam had the ability to rattle me. We were like oil and water. He loved obscure historical facts, nonfiction, and getting under my skin. He claimed that mysteries were fluffy, mind candy meant to be consumed by a less *discerning* readership. However, after we'd teamed up to help Dr. Caldwell and the Redwood Grove police department capture a killer this past summer, I realized Liam had a penchant for sleuthing. He might not admit it openly, but he took as much pleasure as I did in piecing together clues, wading through witness statements, and trying to outwit and outmaneuver a murderer. Unfortunately, our last case had left me with a short stint in the hospital, bruised and sore but not permanently harmed. That hadn't stopped Liam from taking responsibility.

"These look fantastic," I said, pointing to the beets and changing the subject. "How are the rest of the courses coming together? Can I help you with anything?"

"In that dress and those heels? No way." Liam removed the lid from the stock pot. "You can be my taste-tester. Give this a try, and tell me if it needs more salt." He dipped a spoon into the soup.

After the appetizers, the next course would feature a

nocturnal salad with dark leafy kale, spinach, and mixed greens topped with grapes, blackberries, and hazelnuts. The soup was a mystery bisque.

I approached the stove and took the spoon from him. The bisque had a golden glow with a blend of warming spices, pungent ginger, and a sweet finish. I closed my eyes and savored the nuanced flavors of butternut squash and pumpkin. "This is like a cup of fall comfort."

"You like it?" Liam studied my face with an intensity that made my neck feel like it was on fire. "Does it need salt, though?"

"I don't think so. I'm not a chef, but it tastes perfect to me. I could eat that entire vat." I wiggled my eyebrows and stood on my toes to peer into the pot.

"Good. The main courses are in the oven. We have the poisoned-apple pork tenderloins and eggplant parmesan with squid ink pasta for a pescatarian option."

"How much fun did you and Pri have with the menu?" I put the soup spoon in the sink.

"She gets the credit." Liam was oddly generous with his praise. "She's done a deadly chocolate mousse and bloody berry tart for dessert."

"Everything's on schedule?" I shifted the conversation in hopes that it might help me maintain better control of my emotions. As always, my role for the event was more analytical —ensuring we had the timing for each course and the three acts for the mystery coordinated.

"It's all good on my end," Liam replied with casual confidence, returning the lid and opening the oven to check on the pork. "Did I hear yelling a few minutes ago?"

"You heard that in here?" I glanced behind us.

"It was pretty hard to miss." He poked the tenderloin with a meat thermometer. "Anything I need to worry about?"

"I don't think so. Well, at least I hope not." I crossed my fingers. "I think it was an isolated incident. One of the guests, Curtis Wright, seems like he's out to cause a scene, but Penny and Ophelia shut him down."

"Oh, I know Curtis. He's one of my regulars." Liam's lips tightened.

"Really?" I was interested in hearing Liam's perspective. "I didn't realize he came into town much. I got the impression he's a bit of a hermit."

Liam studied the temperature gauge and nodded to himself. He closed the oven and returned his attention to me. His steady, unwavering eye contact made it feel like the kitchen floor was rocking. "You're right. He is, but he's a big WWII buff. He comes out for trivia night. I'm not surprised that he's stirring the pot. That's his MO."

"What do you mean?" I surveyed the kitchen. Penny had done a complete overhaul, restoring the room to its original glory. The large butcher-block island was the central feature, complete with a copper rack hanging above it to display shiny pots and pans. The cabinets had been painted a soft cream and intentionally scuffed to give them a lived-in effect. Open shelves lined the wall next to the pantry displaying ceramic mugs, Mason jars with canned fruits and jams, and vintage cookware.

"He intentionally picks fights. He likes to say things that are controversial just to get a rise out of the other trivia players."

"Huh. Interesting. Sounds exactly like someone I know." I tilted my head to the side and gave him a hard stare.

He shifted his chin letting his hair fall away and giving me a pleading look with his dark eyes that softened. "Hey, Annie, listen, I thought we were past that. How many scones do I have to bake for you to make amends for teasing you about mysteries?"

"Well, I do enjoy your scones, so I'm going to say that the answer to that question is indefinite for the moment." I winked. I enjoyed our playful banter, and Liam's scones were incredibly delicious—buttery, flaky, yet tender and soft. They were a metaphor for his personality, tough on the outside with a pillowy center.

He started to respond, but Penny rushed into the kitchen and slammed the dining room door behind her. She ground her teeth together and yanked open a cupboard. "Where's the booze? I need wine—stat!"

"For you or the guests?" I joked, trying to keep things light.

"Both." Penny dabbed sweat from her forehead with the back of her hand. "They're starting to stream in. We decided to open the doors early because it's a freaking monsoon out there. Everyone is already drenched, and I don't think a soggy dining experience will encourage anyone to open their pockets, so let's get them tipsy instead."

"A little buzz never hurts when it comes to charity auctions." Liam pointed to the fridge. "The white is chilling, and I have the red lined up with extra glasses, in case you need them, over there for you." He motioned to the counter space near the island.

It was refreshing to see him trying to put her at ease.

"Oh, good." Penny glided across the floor on her four-inch heels. I was impressed she could move so gracefully. Whenever I wore heels, a rarity, I felt awkward and clunky, like I had to be hyper-focused on each step I took. She uncorked a bottle of California Cabernet and poured herself a glass of wine, filling it to the brim. Then she took a long swig, standing perfectly still and closing her eyes. "Okay, that's better. I can face this."

"Do you want me to help pour?" I asked. I didn't want to say anything, but I was worried about her. Even before the incident with Curtis, she seemed on edge. If I could help relieve some of her stress by pouring wine or whatever else she needed, I was all in.

"Sure. I want to greet each guest individually, but if you could pour the Chardonnay, that would be very helpful. I'll start with the red and work my way around the table." She took another big sip as if for courage and then picked up two bottles of wine. "Let's do this."

I retrieved bottles of the white from the fridge. The dining room was a sea of bright colors and bedazzled costumes. People huddled in front of the fire and chattered happily. Guests had outdone themselves. I felt proud about that. I had pushed the idea of encouraging guests to come in costume or fancy attire. Penny hadn't been as convinced, but I assured her that locals would relish an opportunity to dress up. Redwood Grove was a laid-back, outdoorsy town, which I loved. I couldn't imagine living anywhere else, but that didn't negate that it was fun to put on something special and elegant every once in a while.

I glanced around and spotted Curtis at the far end of the dining room. He appeared to be behaving, at least temporarily. He was caught up in a conversation with Ophelia. I couldn't hear what they were talking about, but at least they weren't at each other's throats. Thank goodness for that.

As I circulated, filling wine glasses, I complimented guests on their costumes. One woman in particular stood out. She wore a floor-length crimson Art Deco gown with a rhinestone, sequined turban hat.

"You look like you belong on the set of a BBC mystery," I said. "Can I fill your glass?"

She held her goblet for me. "Thank you, dearest. You're adorable with those snakes. I'm Trishelle, by the way. Trishelle Wilder."

"Nice to meet you. I'm Annie Murray. I work at the Secret Bookcase. We're helping to host tonight's fundraiser and have some exciting twists and turns planned for you."

"The Secret Bookcase is still in business, really? That's a shocker. It was a relic even back in my day." Trishelle waved her hand to signal me that her glass was full enough. "I adored that store as a kid. All the cozy nooks and crannies. Here's what I've always wanted to know—there has to be a secret passageway inside, right?"

"Not that I know of," I replied honestly. "We do have a bookcase that opens to reveal a secret room, though."

"No, no. All of these old estates had passageways and tunnels. I'm sure this house does. Your store must, too." She tapped her finger on the table and narrowed her eyes at me like she thought I was lying.

"You'll have to ask Hal, the owner. Maybe he knows something I don't." I kept it light, not wanting to get into a debate about the existence or lack thereof of old passageways in the bookstore since there were plenty of other wine glasses to fill. If I went down that rabbit hole, I might end up talking Trishelle's ear off all night.

Fletcher and I had both spent more time than I cared to admit searching for the rumored secret passages in the estate. I was greatly intrigued by the idea of discovering a hidden corridor or stairway. Penny, Pri, and I had pored over schematics of the farmhouse when she moved in, hoping to stumble upon missing square footage or a closet that didn't match the architectural blueprints. Thus far, we'd been unsuccessful in our quest, but Redwood Grove lore was rich with stories of secret passages and hidden tunnels.

Something caught her attention on the other side of the room. "Excuse me, one moment." She ended our conversation abruptly, slipped away, and made a beeline for Curtis. I watched her walk with a purpose, past the sideboard buffet cabinet, her dress rustling with each step.

She whispered something to Ophelia, who nodded vigorously and stepped away from Curtis, sweeping her hand in his direction, like she was about to make a formal introduction.

Then I blinked twice because I was sure my eyes were failing me. The next thing I knew, Trishelle stalked straight up to him and proceeded to slap him across the face.

THREE

Trishelle swiveled on her heels and strolled back to the fire like nothing had happened. Curtis glared at her with hard, glassy eyes, but otherwise, he didn't react to the slap. You would have thought she had shared her grandmother's recipe for peach jam with him with both of their nonchalant responses to the assault. The rest of the guests glanced around the crowded dining room, trying to decipher whether this was part of the performance.

Pri met my eyes across the table and mouthed, "What should we do?"

I lifted my hands in confusion. An uncomfortable quiet fell over the room like everyone was waiting to see what would happen next. There was no next act because this wasn't in my script. The actors hadn't even made their way into the dining room yet.

Fortunately Penny took change. She picked up a soup spoon and clinked it on the side of her goblet. "Let me be the first to welcome you to the newly restored Wentworth manor. I hope your journey through the storm wasn't too perilous, but I do need to warn you that as the night progresses, I cannot guarantee your safety. Consider this your warning to proceed with caution. Many of you are likely well aware of the Wentworth family's tragic history. I certainly hope that history won't repeat itself tonight. Since I've purchased the property, I have learned that shadows speak in whispers in every corridor. As much as I've tried to ignore their calling while ripping down the siding and tearing out old carpet, I'm afraid the ghosts of Redwood Grove's distant past linger and lurk. Will they make an appearance tonight?" She paused for effect.

Someone let out an "ooohhhh."

The lights flickered in perfect timing.

A woman standing near me startled and let out a little scream.

"There's our answer." Penny lifted her hand toward the chandeliers. "Now, if you'll find your seats, I believe our first course awaits us. As we dine beneath the watchful eyes of those long since departed, I advise you to pay careful attention, trust no one, question everything, and most importantly, keep your wits about you." With that, she tipped her wine glass, took a drink, and sat down.

Everyone applauded. I was impressed with Penny's performance. We hadn't discussed adding a paranormal element, but her welcome speech bumped up the creepy factor and blended beautifully with the wild weather. The thought that old ghosts were joining us for dinner gave me a little shiver.

I helped guests find their place cards, keeping one eye on Curtis. He took his spot at the head of the table and puffed out his chest like he was the king of the evening. He ignored the woman to his left, who was attempting to get his attention to pass the basket of rolls.

I watched as he topped off his wine and then took a big swig. He swished it around in his mouth and sat back, watching everyone with an odd level of anticipation, like he knew a secret he wasn't planning to share.

What was he plotting?

I didn't like his sly smile or the way he lorded it over the table, but aside from disrupting the meal and being rude to other guests, I couldn't imagine that the grumpy old man would be able to put a dampener on dinner.

Ignoring him was probably our best strategy. If Curtis was looking for attention, then we'd do the opposite.

I made a mental note to check in on him routinely. If Penny was right about him wanting to sabotage the dinner, I needed to stay one step ahead of him.

I found my seat. A man in his early fifties with salt-and-pepper hair, full cheeks, and a round chin extended his hand in greeting. "Looks like we're seatmates. I'm Patrick Zimmerman."

Ah, so this was the notorious real estate developer. He wore a black-and-white pin-striped 1930s mobster-style suit. His costume was punctuated with a sharp white tie and a silk red handkerchief in his breast pocket. A thin mustache curled above his upper lip. I couldn't tell if it was real or fake, and I had to resist the urge to tug at it as I shook his hand.

"Nice to meet you, I'm Annie," I said, not mentioning that his name had already come up.

"What brings you to our mysterious dinner?" Patrick asked, unfolding his napkin and placing it on his lap.

"I'm a friend of Penny's. I helped organize the event."

"Wonderful. Splendid. I do enjoy a dinner party. Throw murder in the mix and count me in." He raised arched brows and bugged out his eyes, attempting to appear sinister. "After all, the mafia is in my blood."

I smiled. Liam came into the room, balancing trays of mini quiches and carpaccio. I tried not to stare at his chiseled arms as he passed around the small bites and chatted with guests. His magnetic ease drew everyone in.

"What's Penny's end goal tonight?" Patrick asked, forcing me to tear my gaze away from Liam. "She can't actually expect to make the kind of cash she needs to keep the orchard and vineyard afloat, can she?"

I was taken aback by his directness, and I had no idea (or, frankly, interest in knowing) what Penny intended to share publicly about her fundraising goals.

"She needs a large amount of capital to overhaul her acreage," Patrick continued, oblivious to my lack of response. "I've offered her a nice out with a package that will set up her well and allow her to keep the house and small garden. As her friend, you could help encourage her to consider my offer. Your generation is so resistant to listening to your elders. You millennials want to do everything your way, and then you're shocked when you can't afford your mortgage payments when you're spending your money on daily lattes and dinners like this."

Our conversation had taken a sharp turn, one I didn't appreciate. He disparaged my entire generation and insulted Penny and me. Don't even get me started on the ridiculous myth that lattes were the reason our generation couldn't afford housing.

I suddenly had a glimmer of empathy for Curtis and clarity as to why Penny was stressed. It was no wonder Curtis didn't want to sell his family farm to this pompous ass, and not surprising that Penny felt extra pressure trying to manage such big personalities while trying to be a gracious host.

"You should tell Penny not to underestimate the value of cash in her hand. With my offer, she can be mortgage-free and still have money to invest. I get the romantic notion of running a vineyard, but take it from me; I'm a successful businessman with years of experience." He smoothed his mustache with his index finger.

Gag.

Who was this guy?

The mobster costume was making more sense. His attitude was straight from the history books.

"A property like this will bleed her dry. Owning a vineyard isn't just about pouring wine in a luxurious tasting room. Do you have any idea what kind of grueling work it entails to tend the vines, harvest grapes, produce, and distribute wine? It's not a smart undertaking for girls like you. I've told Penny multiple times that her best move is to accept my offer, cut her losses, and walk away with a nice nest egg."

Girls like us?

We were grown women.

I wanted to punch Patrick in the throat. His condescending, dismissive attitude made me even more resolved to do whatever I could to help Penny keep the farm.

"What would you do with the vineyard and orchard?" I asked, already knowing what his answer would be, but I was doing my best to remain professional and I couldn't think of another way to keep him talking without adding a nasty retort about his inherent sexism. Penny needed tonight to be a success, and after speaking with Patrick for five minutes, I had even more resolve to help her with her plight.

"I don't know if you're aware of this. Land is at a premium in the great state of California." He spoke to me like I was a toddler. "Your generation is upset about affordable housing; well, this is an opportunity to be part of the solution. I have plans for a subdivision for single-family homes with shared amenities—tennis courts, a pool, a community room, and a gym. A girl like Penny would be much better off to have neighbors nearby. She wouldn't be alone out this way in the middle of a bunch of old, rundown farms."

"Would the housing be low-income? Affordable for whom?" I pressed my thumb and index finger to keep from responding to his ongoing condescension toward Penny. I couldn't resist asking the semi-passive aggressive question. There was no chance Patrick was planning on building affordable housing.

People like me, working in retail, or Pri, working in a coffee shop, would be priced out of Patrick's build. Buzzwords like "affordable housing" were tossed around in the negotiating process, but when it came to listing the new houses, they would be astronomically priced, like the rest of California, because that's what "the market demanded." I wasn't buying Patrick's pitch.

"You realize we're in one of the hottest real estate markets in the country." He adjusted his gangster tie. "Affordability is relative, but the only way housing prices will stabilize is if we have more inventory to offer. That's land like this, and the other orchards nearby come in. It's wasted, unused space right now."

I could argue the importance of keeping natural wild spaces and how the farming land surrounding Redwood Grove protected our ecosystem, but I wasn't interested in debating Patrick.

Liam passed by us with a new tray of appetizers. His apron was cinched around his waist like a waiter at a French restaurant. He held the platter easily with one hand at a ninety-degree angle. "Quiche?"

Thank goodness. Saved by food. And Liam Donovan.

I released the grip on my hands and helped myself to a bacon and herb and a tomato and cheese quiche.

"Only two?" Liam's eyes danced as he leaned closer to offer me the tray.

I looked up at him and patted my stomach. "I'm pacing myself. It's a five-course dinner."

Liam placed two more dainty quiches on my plate. "They're bite-sized. You have to try each flavor at least. I need to know which ones are best because I'm considering putting them on the menu at the Stag Head."

"Okay, if you insist." I grinned, biting into cheesy tomato quiche. It was rich yet airy with bright notes of oven-roasted tomatoes and finished with a hint of rosemary sea salt. "Delicious," I said through a mouthful.

"Report back later." He moved on to continue passing the appetizers.

I felt a twinge of regret that I hadn't thought of something cleverer to say, and I tried not to stare at him while he served other guests. His magnetic pull made it nearly impossible. Twice, he caught me staring at him and smiled at me playfully. I hoped that everyone around me, including him, assumed the flush on my cheeks was from the wine.

Ophelia slipped into the seat on the other side of me. I was relieved to be able to shift my conversation away from Patrick and distract myself from Liam's handsome, chiseled jawline.

"Is everything ready?" I asked her, noticing that three of the other actors had taken their seats. Jeff would join in to deliver the soup course as our fake chef. The detective and victim were seated across the table from me on either side of Trishelle.

"Nothing ever goes without a few hiccups on opening night, but all things considered, I'm feeling good about where we're at. This group of players has gelled well as a cast, which is half the battle, frankly, especially when it comes to improv."

"Glad to hear it." I nibbled on the quiches, sipping my wine and watching people chat around the table. When I studied criminology in college, we spent hours observing body language and behavior. Dr. Caldwell, my professor, had encouraged us to bring a notebook and a pen and blend into the background at a very public location like a coffee shop or library.

"As detectives, you'll need to hone your observation skills," she would say to the class, peering at us from her oversized black glasses. "Take copious notes. What do you see? Can you pick up on a stranger's tell? Can you identify who's arguing or ogling another customer?"

Ever since, it has been a game I like to play with myself.

Could I discern what was happening without overhearing a conversation or lip reading?

For the most part, our guests appeared lighthearted. Wine flowed freely, and a sense of comradery and eager anticipation filled the room. Everyone knew why they were here. A murder was going to occur. The question was when? And who was the unsuspecting victim?

FOUR

The action began as Jeff introduced the next course, while Liam stood waiting with trays of steaming soup.

"Uh, everyone. Uh, I'd like to give you some tasting notes for our next course,'" Jeff said in a voice that was barely audible. He spoke to the floor, circling his left foot on the rug.

No one paid any attention.

Ophelia motioned for him to look up and project.

He tugged on his starched white chef's coat and spoke to the floor. "Um, ladies and gentlemen, if I could have a minute of your time. I'm your chef tonight and I have tasting notes to share with you."

His voice was faint over the din of conversations.

Ophelia waved her arms, encouraging him to bring more energy. She turned to me and muttered out of the side of her mouth, "I take back what I said. I don't know why I cast him in this role. He's scared of his own shadow. I should have made him the victim, but his death scene was dreadful. It was the saddest, most pathetic thing I've ever seen."

"Do you want me to get everyone's attention?" I asked, reaching for my wine glass.

"No. No. He's in character. He needs to own that he's a head chef. It works with the material if he's a bit nervous. Most chefs aren't comfortable speaking with patrons, but he needs to project." Ophelia shook her finger at him like she was scolding a child. She cupped her hands over her lips and mouthed, "Project."

"Speak up or shut up, kid," Curtis blurted out.

I didn't even realize he was paying attention, especially because he was as far away from Jeff as you could get.

Jeff blew out air in long bursts like he was trying not to hyperventilate. Then he cleared his throat loudly and stomped his foot on the floor.

That did the trick. People stopped talking and turned toward him.

"Welcome to Wentworth, ladies and gentlemen. I'm Jeff, your head chef this evening, and I'll be discussing each course before it's served." His voice was wobbly, but he found more confidence as he continued. "The appetizers were handcrafted in a murderous melody of textures—carpaccio in the form of bloody beets." He spoke like a Michelin-star chef reviewing the menu with expectant guests. This was more in line with the self-important character I had written for him. "You likely met my sous chef during the appetizer course." He motioned to Liam with a dismissive flick of the wrist. "I hope you enjoyed our interpretation of some delectable bites."

A smattering of applause broke out.

Jeff acknowledged the praise with a bob of his head. I could tell he was connecting more to the character as he began explaining how he (technically Liam) had prepared the bisque. "I invite you to put your palates and taste buds to the test and see if you can correctly identify the flavors in our soup course. I'll tell you that the bisque is layered and puréed, but it's up to you to solve the mystery of the ingredients in the soup." He removed a quarter sheet of cream paper from his pocket. "You'll find tasting notes on each of your plates. Use them to record what you pull out of each course. I believe there will be a prize for whoever correctly identifies all of the courses at the night's end." He looked at Penny for confirmation.

She stood. "Yes, thank you, Chef."

Jeff bowed and stepped back into the kitchen.

"While Chef and his team deliver our bisque, I'll top off wine." She moved to the buffet and picked up a bottle of white and red.

"He's no chef," Curtis scoffed, slurring his words slightly. His wine glass sat empty. He must have chugged his drink. Mine was still nearly full. "If this is the quality of the acting we're getting tonight, I want my money back. I want a refund. I was promised murder. Where's the murder?"

Ophelia clutched her chest. "Someone shut that old windbag up before he ruins everything."

The actor playing the victim jumped out of her seat, spilled her wine, and stood on her chair. "Did you see that? Who did it? Who did it?"

"Did what?" the actor playing the detective on the other side of Trishelle asked, completely perplexed.

"A spider. There's a spider in my drink," she shrieked, waving wildly at the spilled wine glass. "Who did it?"

"A spider in your drink?" the actor asked, peering closer and then gasping as he picked up her goblet and held it for the entire table to see. "She's right."

What was going on? "That wasn't in the script," I whispered to Ophelia. The actor, still standing on her chair, was soon to meet an untimely death, but not until she had slurped Chef's poisoned soup.

"Ah, the art of misdirection." Ophelia gave me a smug smile. "Improvisation at its best."

"Love it." The distraction had worked.

"Look what you've done. You've spilled on my dress. It's

ruined." Trishelle pushed her chair away from the table and hurried to the buffet for a fresh napkin.

Curtis was silenced. Penny refilled his wine glass to the brim. She leaned in close and said something in his ear that made him turn ghostly white.

Good for her. Hopefully, she had put him in his place. Or given him a final warning. It wasn't fair to the rest of the guests and those of us who had poured long hours into preparations. I was sure we could recruit Liam to escort Curtis outside if it came down to it.

Trishelle dabbed her dress with a handful of napkins, making a big show of trying to wipe away an invisible stain. She returned to her seat, blotting her dress with a soggy napkin.

Jeff and Liam delivered steaming bowls of creamy bisque. I enjoyed watching guests savor each bite, closing their eyes or swishing the soup around on their palate and then making frantic notes on their tasting sheets. I knew I had insider information, but the pumpkin and squash came through with each taste.

When Jeff placed a bowl of soup in front of Curtis, Curtis slapped his hand on Jeff's wrist, clasping it with a death grip. "We're not done, son. I told you I wanted a word, and you're not getting out of here until we finish what *you* started."

Jeff gulped, trying unsuccessfully to free himself from Curtis's grasp. "Sir, if you have any comments about the food, please share them on your comment cards."

"Get a load of this kid," Curtis bellowed, dropping Jeff's wrist like he had a contagious disease. "I wouldn't quit your day job."

Jeff tucked the empty soup tray under his arm and scurried away.

"It should be any minute now," Ophelia said, tapping on a thin silver watch. "We're on schedule and ready for the big scene. This is the moment when my nerves begin to bubble up as a director. We've logged hours and lines, brainstormed different scenarios, and now I have to sit back and hope my young starlets shine bright."

Her energy was palpable. Even though I knew what was coming, a buzzing sensation spread down my body. I was eager to see how the actor was going to pull off her death scene. Would she take a subtle approach, slumping in her chair? Or would she go for over-the-top theatrics? Maybe falling to her knees or stumbling around the table?

If guests were having this much fun trying to guess soup flavors, I couldn't wait to see their reaction to the fake murder. In the mystery I'd written, the victim is poisoned, and the chef is the most likely suspect since he had access to her soup and hand-delivered it to the table. But, as with any good mystery, the first and most likely suspect could have an alibi or a reasonable explanation as to why they couldn't possibly be the killer. It would be the job of the guests to work together, share information, and figure out the true culprit by the end of the evening.

Knowing what was about to happen made it hard to sit still. I didn't want to be too obvious and keep my eyes on the actor who was about to die, but I didn't want to miss it either. Was anyone at the table paying close enough attention to notice a sleight of hand, a last-minute switch?

Was the poison in her soup? Or had the killer crafted another plan?

I enjoyed the hearty bisque and people-watching. Silverware clattered, and the din in the room grew louder as more wine was consumed. Laughter and music filled the air as everyone tucked into their soup and studied their seatmates, waiting to see who was about to drop dead.

The actor playing the victim held her soup spoon to her lips. Her eyes started to flutter.

This was it.

But before she could fake her starting scene, Curtis pushed

back his chair and stumbled to his feet, clutching his neck and wheezing. Ugly red splotches spread from his chest to his face. He gasped like a fish out of water.

"Eek," a woman across the table squealed with delight and fanned her face. "It's happening."

But it wasn't.

Curtis wasn't the intended victim.

Why was he pretending to choke?

Was this another one of his attempts to sabotage the dinner?

"Stop it, Curtis," Ophelia demanded, making a slicing motion across her neck.

He sputtered and fell backward into the buffet; his hand swiped an empty wine bottle, toppling it over. It shattered on the floor.

"I don't think he's acting," someone shouted.

Everything suddenly came into sharp focus. They were right. This wasn't part of the script. Curtis wasn't involved in the plot. My breath caught in my chest. A sour taste filled my mouth.

Curtis was in trouble. I jumped to my feet, knocking over my chair.

The energy shifted. People looked around wildly for help as Curtis's face swelled like an overly filled balloon about to pop.

Without hesitation, I raced over to help. I was trained in CPR and first aid.

Curtis's breathing was shallow and rapid. His heartbeat pounded so fast and hard I could see it in his chest.

This wasn't good.

This wasn't normal.

"Call 911," I said to Pri, who hovered nearby just as Curtis grabbed my chest and yanked me closer.

"Poison," he said through a fading breath, and then he collapsed.

FIVE

I tried to revive him. "Curtis, Curtis, stay with me." I loosened his collar and checked his airway. My training kicked in. I methodically went through each step. Nothing was obstructing his breathing. His heart had stopped. I lowered him to the floor to start chest compressions. I could hear Pri talking to emergency services, but the room around me went blurry. It was like my mind weeded out any and all distractions to allow me to laser in on the task of trying to breathe life back into Curtis's limp body.

The farmhouse was at least a fifteen-minute drive from town. I wondered how long it would take first responders to arrive.

"Annie, we have a problem," Pri said with the phone still pressed to her ear. "Apparently, there are a bunch of trees down, blocking the road. Crews are on the scene, but it's going to be a while before they make it here."

My stomach sunk like I had been dropped from the top of a rollercoaster.

"They want to speak with you." She handed me the phone.

Dispatch asked me dozens of questions designed to assess

whether continuing CPR made sense. I already knew it didn't, but I couldn't just stop.

"Annie." Pri kneeled beside me and softly placed a hand on my shoulder. "He's gone."

"I know, but..." I couldn't finish my sentence. Admitting that Curtis was dead and there was nothing we could do to save him felt too heavy. My arms quivered as I kept pumping his chest.

If only the rescuers could get here. I could keep going. I could save him.

No, you can't, Annie. He's gone.

My rational brain began to win out.

"It's time to stop." Pri squeezed my shoulder tighter.

I knew she was right, but it went against every instinct to just give up.

The sour taste spread over my tongue. I fought back the urge to gag. This couldn't be happening. Not tonight. Not in the middle of our dinner party. Everything had been so thoroughly planned. I felt terrible for Penny, for Pri, and most importantly for Curtis.

I knew enough from my time as a criminology student that Curtis hadn't died of natural causes. This wasn't a heart attack or choking. The splotches on his neck and face, the way he gasped for air, and the fact that his last word had been "poison" made me sure that he had been murdered. Why?

His death was uncannily similar to the plot I had written. Had the killer taken advantage of that?

A death by poison was supposed to occur tonight, only the poison we had procured for our little show was a vial of almond syrup that Pri used to craft layered chocolate almond mochas at Cryptic.

Did that point to someone on the cast being the killer?

Could they have taken my script and rewritten it?

I let Pri help me to my feet, unable to tear my gaze away from Curtis's puffy, lifeless face.

Liam suddenly appeared behind me. Had he been there the whole time? "You okay, Annie?" he asked gently. His eyes mirrored my denial.

I wanted to collapse in his steady arms.

Tears welled behind my eyes. I fought them back and forced a nod.

"We're going to need to move the body," he said in a low tone, not wanting to call more attention to the scene, offering me his hand.

Standing sent waves of tiny lights across my vision. Was I going to black out?

Pri steadied my arm. "You're okay, Annie. Take a slow breath."

I did as she directed, inhaling through my nose and shutting my eyes tight to try to force the spots out of my vision. When I opened my eyes again, the room looked crisper, like I'd polished my glasses. Guests sat frozen in their seats. All eyes were directed at us, like we were performers on stage.

"This isn't part of the act, is it?" A woman covered her mouth with a napkin like she was going to be sick. I didn't blame her. My stomach swirled with nervous energy as a chill spread down my arms.

Penny clutched the wine bottle she'd been using to refill drinks in one hand and addressed the guests. Her voice wobbled, but she held a firm stance. "As I'm sure you're all very well aware, this is not part of our dinner theater. A horrific accident has occurred."

An audible gasp rippled around the table.

One guest burst into tears.

Another clutched his fork like he was preparing to fight off a potential attack.

I wasn't so sure it was an accident, but there was no need to worry anyone. At least not yet.

"Obviously, this is not what we expected or intended. There has been a terrible tragedy," Penny continued, her voice shrill and shaky. "Before we determine what to do next, I think the most appropriate thing to do is to take a moment of silence to honor Curtis."

Everyone fell still.

I was glad that Penny had suggested taking a pause. I needed to wrap my head around what our next steps should be, and I also needed a minute to get my emotions in check. Freaking out could wait. I had to keep it together and remain professional in the short term.

"Thank you for that," Penny said, keeping her hand glued to the wine bottle like it was a security blanket.

A log slipped in the fireplace, sending sparks and embers shooting up the chimney.

I clutched my chest at the sound of it thudding against the hearth.

I knew it was expected to be jumpy in a situation like this, but being skittish wasn't going to help bring Curtis's assailant to justice.

You have one job now, Annie.

Figure out who poisoned him and how.

And keep them detained until the authorities arrive.

Okay, technically, that was three jobs, but they were all connected.

"What happened?" Jeff interrupted my thoughts. I couldn't tell if he was addressing me or anyone who would listen. He stood next to the kitchen door, holding an empty tray under his arm.

The bisque.

Curtis had become ill after the soup course.

Could the poison have been in the bisque?

But then, wouldn't we all be sick? Everyone at the table had consumed the soup. I felt fine.

I scanned the table, searching for any signs that someone else might be unwell. Guests were rightfully upset. People fidgeted. Patrick ran his hands on his pant legs repeatedly. Ophelia twisted the bracelets on her wrists like they were toys. Trishelle crossed her arms over her stomach in a protective huddle. Jeff looked pale and sickly, but no one was gasping for air or turning beet red.

If it had been the bisque, Curtis must have been specifically targeted.

Who had access to the kitchen? My mind began mapping the scene and everything leading up to the death.

Liam, obviously, had been in the kitchen the entire night, but I could rule him out. He might err on the side of pompousness, but he wasn't a killer. Not to mention that he had no motive for wanting Curtis dead.

But Jeff was another story. As our chef actor, Jeff was the only other person allowed in the kitchen. Curtis had demanded to speak with Jeff in the living room earlier, and Jeff had obviously been unsettled, hence chewing his collar and trying to make himself small. And then there was their nasty exchange when Jeff served Curtis's soup. What could it mean?

I needed to find out as much as I could about their backstory and connection.

"Was it a heart attack?" Ophelia asked, leaning over the table to get a better look at Curtis's body. Her bracelets jangled against her wine glass, nearly knocking it over.

"I don't know," I answered less than truthfully. "The authorities will have to determine the cause of death."

"I know exactly what happened. He's pretending to be poisoned. Curtis is the most exasperating man on the planet. I'm so tired of his antics." Ophelia threw her hand to the back of her forehead and fell into her chair. "This is too much.

What utter nonsense. Curtis probably slipped himself something to ruin our performance. Trying to upstage my actors again. Have you checked his vitals? He's probably playing dead."

Upstage her actors? That was a stretch.

I almost wanted to offer her a chance to get a good look at the boils on his skin, but I wasn't going to risk anyone else contaminating the crime scene or panicking the other guests.

The problem was that if it was really going to take the police an hour or more to arrive, we couldn't sit in the same room with the body. I had to take charge. I was the most qualified person, at least for the time being.

I considered our options. We could move Curtis carefully to another area in the house and preserve his place setting, or we could move the entire party to the living room and cordon off the dining room.

The latter required more moving parts and more opportunities for the killer, who had to be among us, to tamper with any potential evidence.

"What are we supposed to do?" the actor who was meant to be the intended victim asked.

Penny's face went blank. She looked at Pri and then at me, squeezing her eyes shut tight and folding her shoulders over. "I don't know. Um, I'm at a loss for words. This doesn't seem real. I don't know—"

That was my cue. I swallowed for courage and inhaled deeply.

This is what you studied. This is what you trained for, Annie.

You know what to do.

"Sadly, I can confirm that Curtis is deceased. This isn't an act. We're going to move him out of the dining room," I said with a confidence I didn't entirely feel. "No one should touch his plate, chair, or anything that Curtis came into contact with."

"Why?" Jeff asked, rubbing a hole in the carpet with his shoe. "It was an accident; why can't we touch anything?"

"It's standard procedure in any investigation," I replied. That much was true. Every crime scene was treated like a homicide until the police could rule out foul play.

"I think she did it," Patrick said, pointing a finger at Penny. "I'm a crime TV connoisseur. That wasn't an accident. Look at his face. Someone killed him, and I've seen enough shows to know that the last person who interacted with the victim is always the killer. She poured his wine minutes before he dropped dead. My bet is that the poison is in that bottle. That's probably why she hasn't set it down."

"What? Me?" Penny gaped at him in shock and then stared at the bottle in her hands like she had no idea how it had gotten there. "You think I killed Curtis?"

Patrick used his napkin to dab the edges of his soup bowl. "I do. I know that Curtis has been trying to get your property. I know that you're holding an empty bottle of wine that you used to fill his glass. I watched him take a drink. You know what happened right after he took a big swig?"

Penny shook her head repeatedly as if she were willing Patrick to stop talking. She pressed the wine bottle to her chest like it was a comfort item.

"Instant death. Whatever you slipped him took him out immediately." Patrick's words were laced with rage. "You killed him right here in front of us, and I watched you do it. Someone should lock her up before she makes a run for it."

"No, I didn't do it." Penny took a step forward but stumbled, catching herself on the edge of the table. "I filled everyone's wine glasses. You saw me do that, too. I circled the entire table." Her eyes were wild as she searched everyone's face, hoping that someone would back her up.

Ophelia raised her glass. "It's true. She filled my wine, and I'm feeling fine."

Patrick folded his napkin into a neat square. "That doesn't mean anything. She probably had the poison in her pocket or hand. She could have slipped it into his glass before she topped it off with the wine."

"I don't even have pockets," Penny protested, running her free hand over her fringe.

This was getting out of hand quickly. We couldn't spend the next hour accusing each other.

"Let's all take a beat," I said. "We don't know what happened. We've done what we can do, and now we need to wait for the authorities. To make everyone more comfortable, we'll move the body. Pri, please find some tape or something to secure Curtis's seat. Everyone else, stay exactly where you are."

"What about dinner?" Jeff asked, pointing to the kitchen.

"We'll deal with that next. Right now, I need a few strong hands to help me." I looked at Liam.

I couldn't believe this was real life, but I felt better doing something. Being stuck in a room with a dead body was only going to make the situation worse. We needed to concentrate on one thing at a time. And right now, that was Curtis.

SIX

"We don't want to disturb the body any more than is necessary," I said quietly to Liam while Pri went to find tape or something to rope off Curtis's seat and place setting. "You brought your own supplies, right? Did you happen to include gloves or large Ziploc bags?"

Liam reached for a fire poker and used it to push the fallen log back away from the hearth. The earthy smell of the sweet wood was oddly comforting. Nothing sounded more appealing at the moment than escaping to the comfort of my cozy cottage and curling up with a mug of cinnamon and cardamom tea with a blanket and a book. I wouldn't mind having Liam snuggled up next to me either, but instead, I had a murder to solve. As much as I wished the circumstances were different, I had to take charge. Dr. Caldwell had recently asked me to join her team. I was still considering her offer, but I was professionally trained with a degree in criminology. I knew what to do, and I was confident in my ability to protect the crime scene and the guests in the short term. This was in my DNA, and I wasn't about to shrink away from my responsibility. Curtis deserved that much.

Plus, the killer had to be one of us. That meant that we were all in danger.

"You should know by now that I overprepare," Liam said, stabbing the log. "I have all of the above and then some."

I almost blurted out, "I love you." That would have been a disaster, but I did love that he came prepared. "Good. That's really good. The first thing we need to do is put on gloves before we move him."

"Where do you want to move him?" Liam asked, deferring to me while gazing around the room, looking for a spot to stash the body.

I hadn't thought that far ahead.

Jeff moved out of the way for us, stepping into the kitchen.

"No, sorry. You need to stay in the dining room with the other guests." I motioned in the other direction. "Everyone is going to need to stay together until the police arrive."

"What if someone needs to use the bathroom?" Jeff asked, switching the empty tray to his other hand.

"We'll cross that bridge when we come to it. For now, please go join the others." The tray was bothering me. It was a long shot, but there was a potential chance that if Jeff had poisoned Curtis, he could have left a residue behind. "Hang on a minute."

I hurried into the kitchen and found the tubs with Liam's supplies near the pantry. I started to lift the lid on the first tub when Liam swooped in to stop me.

"I've got it." He bumped me out of the way and then blocked my view of the tub. "I'll get them."

"Okay." Why was he acting so weird? They were just gloves.

He rifled through the tub, pulling out cleaning supplies and resting them on the floor as he searched for the gloves.

I could have sworn I caught a glimpse of a vintage book with a soft green cover and gilded pages, but Liam shoved it into the bottom of the tub before I could get a better look.

He handed me a pair of oversized yellow dishwashing gloves and snapped the lid back on the tub before I could see what he was keeping from me.

The gloves were way too big for me, but they would have to do. I slid them over my fingers, feeling like I did when I used to help in our family diner as a kid. "Let me take that tray from you," I said, carefully lifting the silver platter from Jeff's arm.

"What are you doing with that?" he asked, sounding nervous. He reached for his collar again, tucking the starched material in his mouth and chewing on it like a fresh stick of minty gum.

"Since you served Curtis's soup, this will need to be included in evidence."

"Evidence?" His eyes bulged. He unfastened the top button of his chef's coat and scratched his neck. "Why?"

I didn't have time to repeat myself. "Don't worry about it. As I said, this is typical protocol. We need to preserve as much of the scene as we can until the authorities can get here. Please join the others."

Liam pulled on a pair of gloves, too. They looked much less ridiculous than mine on his large hands. "What now, Detective Murray?"

"What do you think about putting him in the pantry?" I nodded toward the kitchen, keeping my voice low. "It's attached to the kitchen but doesn't have an outside exit. That way, if we contain the guests in the dining room, there's no danger of anyone disturbing the body." It was probably far-fetched to worry about that, but then again, I never would have expected a real murder to occur during our dinner party.

"Works for me." Liam lifted Curtis from behind, linking his arms under Curtis's shoulders.

I took his feet, acutely aware that all eyes were on us. "I

know this is disturbing," I said to the guests. "Try to remain calm. We're going to move him somewhere safe, and then we'll figure out next steps." I was surprised by how calm I sounded.

Curtis wasn't a heavy man, but lifting the dead weight made my muscles seize, and that was with Liam carrying the bulk of his body. He kicked the door to the kitchen open with his foot and shuffled inside.

"Do you want to proceed with dinner?" He didn't sound winded as we dragged Curtis past the island where dozens of beautifully plated salads waited to be delivered. "It would be a shame to have this food go to waste, but I'll follow your lead, Annie."

"Yeah, I think it would be best to continue with dinner. I mean, we'll scrap the murder plot, but depending on how long it takes for the police to show up, people might start to go stir-crazy. The more we can keep everyone calm and collected, the better." I felt like if Dr. Caldwell were here, she would say the same thing.

"But you don't think he had a heart attack," Liam said, shifting Curtis's weight to one side in order to open the pantry door. He walked backward until we'd managed to get his body into the small storage room.

The pantry was on the backside of the kitchen. It was a small space, about eight feet long by three feet wide. Sturdy whitewashed wooden shelves stretched from the floor to the ceiling. They were thoughtfully stocked with glass jars of dried herbs, spices, and preserves. Penny had handwritten labels and organized items alphabetically.

"No. I think Ophelia's right that he ingested something that killed him almost instantly." I tried to think back through the minutes before Curtis began gasping for air. I'd finished my soup, and Penny was refilling wine. The actor playing the victim discovered the spider in her drink. Trishelle got up to clean her dress, but so did the actor playing the detective. Jeff was serving the soup. I hadn't noticed what Patrick and Ophelia were doing because I'd been distracted by the spider. Was that the killer's plan?

How fast-acting was the poison? Maybe there was also a chance that he'd been poisoned much earlier in the evening, and the drug was slower acting. I didn't know enough about poisons to speak with any kind of authority.

"That doesn't look good for Penny." Liam propped Curtis's back against the far shelves, which were lined with canned tomatoes, peaches, and pears. It was a strange juxtaposition—Penny's homey canning and Curtis's lifeless body. My mind couldn't quite make sense of it. It was like living in a bizarre dream, or better yet—a nightmare.

"She couldn't have killed him," I insisted, resting his feet on the cold black and white checkerboard floor.

"I'm not saying she did it." Liam paused like he was trying to find the right words. "I *am* saying it doesn't look good for her. You're going to need to take the wine bottle, too. You realize that, right?"

I had been thinking the same thing. On a personal level, I was sure that Penny wasn't involved in Curtis's murder, but on a professional level, I knew I had to treat everyone like a potential suspect, for her sake, as much as anything.

"Yeah." I waited for Liam to step around Curtis's body, and then we shut the pantry door. "I'll do that now. Do you want to pass out salads?"

He hesitated. "Sure, but do we need to consider that the killer could have poisoned them, too? The plates have been on the island for twenty minutes. I was waiting to finish them with the balsamic reduction right before we served them."

I thought about the possibility for a minute. Could we have a serial killer on our hands? Doubtful. If that were the case surely one of us would be exhibiting symptoms by now.

Curtis had made an impression, and not a good one. I had

the sense that this was a targeted attack. "My gut says it's fine, but what do you think?"

I couldn't believe that Liam and I were teaming up. It was nice to have someone to bounce ideas off of, but whenever Liam Donovan was near, the rational side of my brain seemed to vanish. Given that there was a dead body locked in the pantry, I needed all of my wits about me tonight.

"I agree." He moved to the sink, rolled his gloves off his muscular arms, and lathered up his hands with soap.

I surveyed the kitchen while I waited for my turn at the sink. My gaze landed on the salads, artfully decorated with rich-toned blackberries and sprigs of rosemary. "Who else has been in the kitchen tonight other than me and Jeff?"

Liam ran his hands under hot water, scrubbing furiously. I wasn't sure if it was because the reality that we had just moved a dead body was sinking in or merely his chef's training. Even with my criminal justice training, I couldn't wait to follow suit and try to wash away any memory of Curtis's pained, puffy face and empty eyes.

"You and Jeff were in and out and a few times. Penny came in right before we served the soup course." Icy rain hit the windows, sounding like hail. The lights flickered again as the wind thrashed outside.

I sighed, letting my shoulders slump. That was not the best-case scenario for Penny. I hadn't noticed her slip away from the table, but then again, I'd been deep in conversation with Ophelia and Patrick. "She did? Do you happen to remember when exactly?"

Liam's arms turned bright red from the water and the force of the scrubbing. "I was wrapped up in prep, so I wasn't paying attention to the clock, but I know it was after Jeff had cleared the appetizer plates."

"What did she do while she was in here?" I wished I had my laptop. While things were fresh, we needed to put together a timeline. It was the first and most critical task when assessing a crime scene.

Liam left the water running and made room for me at the sink. "I'm not sure. I think that she grabbed more wine, but I was basting the pork loin and had my back to her. Whatever she did must not have taken long because, by the time I closed the oven, she was already gone."

I slipped off my gloves and ran my hands under the scalding water, not caring that it burned. Cleansing my hands literally and figuratively gave me a minute to collect my thoughts and figure out our next steps. "Is there paper or a pen in here anywhere?"

Liam dried his hands on a towel and opened a drawer on the far side of the sink. He riffled through it until he found a spiral-bound notebook and pen. "Will this work?"

"Perfect." I brushed my hands together vigorously and turned off the water. "Let's start from the beginning." I took the notebook from him and made a long line down the center of the first sheet of paper.

"How far is the beginning? Before guests arrived?" Liam picked up a container of balsamic and shook it lightly, using his finger as a stopper. "I'm going to dress the salads while you write. As far as time goes, Penny let me in at four p.m. to begin prep. She and Pri were the only people here then."

"Okay." I made a little dot at the start of the line and noted Liam's arrival. "I showed up about a half hour after you. Ophelia and the actors were here at six to warm up. The question is, when exactly did Curtis sneak inside? He was supposed to be outside with the other guests, but he must have found a way in earlier because he was fighting with Ophelia in the living room. I never checked whether the doors were locked. Everyone else was queued in the rain, so how did he get in? Did he simply open the door, or could he have come in around the back?"

"No idea. I've been in the kitchen this entire time." Liam drizzled balsamic dressing on a salad.

I flipped to the next page and made a list of questions. Then I returned to my timeline. "Penny officially opened the doors to guests at seven, and appetizers were served right as people entered the dining room."

"Yep. We served the soup at seven-thirty." Liam pointed to a small whiteboard propped up against the counter. Like a true professional, he had mapped out timing for each course to coincide with the script. Dishes were slotted to be served in thirty-minute increments to give guests enough time to savor their food and for the actors to engage in their roles. "And the salad was due to go out at eight, but obviously, we're behind schedule now."

"Right." I jotted the times down. "Jeff was in the kitchen for the duration of prep. Is that correct?" I felt more centered working the problem and analyzing the facts. I was barely distracted by Liam's sultry eyes. My brain snapped into focus, tapping into years of cellular memory and training.

Liam used a paper towel to wipe the edge of a salad plate clean. "He hung around, but again, he's not a trained chef and doesn't have his food handler's permit, so basically, he stood near the door like a skittish cat just waiting for his cue."

"But he helped you serve the appetizers and the soup." I made a note of Jeff's whereabouts.

"Yes." He finished the last salad and began placing them on trays.

"Walk me through that. I'm assuming what you're doing right now is what happened with the soup? You ladled bowls, put them on the trays, and Jeff carried them out to the dining room? Did he have any other contact with food?"

"Nope. This might be a private catering gig, but the same rules apply. Jeff was acting as a chef, but he was a glorified server tonight."

"And there's no chance he touched or tampered with the vat of soup?" I doodled on the edge of the page.

"None." Liam shook his head with confidence. "That's not to say that he couldn't have slipped something into Curtis's bowl. He definitely delivered at least two trays of soup to guests."

I thought back to how Curtis had grabbed Jeff's wrist and threatened him when Jeff served his soup. "Did you see Jeff slip anything into Curtis's bowl?"

Liam paused for a minute. I appreciated that he was taking this seriously. "No, Curtis was sitting at the end of the table farthest away from the kitchen. I wasn't paying attention, sorry."

"It's okay. I didn't see anything either. It was a long shot." I noted that as well. "But Penny came into the kitchen before the soup went out?"

He picked up a tray. "Yes. I know it was before the soup was served because I was in the middle of dishing up the bisque when my basting timer went off. I had to stop for a minute to check on the pork before I finished ladling the soup."

One huge benefit to having Liam's input on the timeline of events was that I trusted his recollection. "That means Penny was likely in the kitchen a few minutes before seven-thirty, as was Jeff. Curtis finished his soup and began experiencing symptoms twenty minutes later. I administered CPR for fifteen minutes, so we're calling the time of death five minutes after eight." I marked those spots on the timeline.

"So you're assuming he was poisoned around seven thirty?" Liam asked, making strong eye contact.

"It looks that way, but we'll have to wait for toxicology reports and the autopsy. I can't say for sure that he was poisoned, and I'm no expert, so it could be that he ingested something much earlier that took longer to interact." I pointed to one of the trays. "Do you want me to help?"

"Sure." Liam balanced two trays and used his foot to kick the door open.

I opted for one. The last thing we needed was for me to spill salads all over the floor.

I felt a bit more in control with getting everything in my head on paper, but I knew we were far from being out of danger. One of the guests I was about to serve had killed Curtis, and I wasn't going to let my guard down until I figured out who had twisted what was supposed to be a fun party into a night of deadly intrigue.

SEVEN

The mood in the dining room was distinctly darker.

"Are the police on their way?" Trishelle asked. She was seated in front of the fireplace with her turban in her lap. "What's taking so long?"

Had she missed everything we'd said before moving Curtis? "They are, but the roads are blocked by downed trees, so it might be a while." I placed a salad in front of Patrick.

"Who's in charge?" Trishelle asked, rocking in her chair. She tipped it precariously close to the fire. "I don't feel comfortable sitting around this table being locked in a room all night with a bunch of strangers."

"I'm in charge," I replied without hesitation. "No one is being locked in here, but we do need to stay together until the authorities arrive and can take everyone's statements."

"What gives you the right to decide you're in charge?" Trishelle questioned, fiddling with the gems on her turban.

I couldn't tell if she was trying to be difficult or if it was her reaction to a highly charged, stressful environment. For the time being, I was willing to give her the benefit of the doubt. I would probably feel the same way if I were in her shoes.

Pri answered for me. "Annie has a degree in criminology. She's assisted the local police with other investigations. We're lucky she's here tonight, and I think it's a good idea if we all listen to her advice."

That shut Trishelle up, at least momentarily.

"I'm assuming you don't want to proceed with our little production?" Ophelia asked as I handed her a salad.

"No." I shook my head and frowned. "Our goal for the remainder of the evening is to keep everyone safe and as comfortable as possible until Dr. Caldwell and the police arrive."

Penny shot me a grateful smile. Her eyes were bloodshot like she'd been crying. I wondered if I had missed something while Liam and I were working through a timeline. Not that I would be surprised or judge her for feeling emotional at a time like this. I felt the same. Seeing death up close was unsettling. My way of channeling the trauma was to concentrate on solving the problem and doing everything in my power to keep us safe.

I passed around the last of the salads.

"So we're supposed to sit and act like there's not a dead guy in the other room. A dead guy that was probably killed by one of us," Patrick asked, holding his fork like a weapon.

"I'm afraid we don't have any other option," I answered truthfully.

Penny stood and addressed the table. Her hair was tousled, and her makeup was streaked from her tears. "I'm terribly, terribly sorry that the evening has taken such an awful turn, but you all generously paid for a delectable meal. Liam, our real chef, has gone out of his way to make a world-class meal for us, and we're in agreement that it would be a shame to let this food go to waste." She brushed an eyelash from her cheek and gave me a pained smile. "Annie has made it clear that leaving isn't a choice until the police get here; I suggest we try to make the best of the situation and at least enjoy these dishes that our chef, Liam, has worked so hard to create for us."

"Chef Liam? I thought Jeff was the head chef." The front legs of Trishelle's chair landed on the floor with a thud. She almost lost her balance but managed to catch herself on the edge of the table. In doing so, she dropped her turban. It went rolling under the table and landed near Patrick's feet. He bent over to pick it up, but Trishelle stopped him. "Don't touch that. The jewelry in my headpiece is extremely valuable."

Patrick stabbed his salad while Trishelle crawled under the table to retrieve her turban. Once she had recovered it, she placed it back on her head, using both hands to ensure it was secure.

"Isn't he the chef?" she repeated, circling her finger in Jeff's direction.

"Are you actually that dense?" Ophelia asked. "He's an actor. He's playing—well, was supposed to play—a chef in our murder mystery."

"Ohhhhh." Trishelle stretched out her response like realization was dawning on her. The crystals in her hat caught the candlelight. I don't own expensive jewelry, but I was fairly sure that those were rhinestones, not actual diamonds. Who would wear diamonds to an event like this? She kicked off her shoes and made figure eights on the floor with her bare feet. "That tall, dark, and handsome guy is the real chef?"

Liam had returned to the kitchen. I wondered how he would have reacted to Trishelle calling him handsome. He probably would have shrugged it off, but still, I couldn't deny feeling a touch of jealousy.

"Liam is the chef," Penny responded. "He's prepared another course after this, and Pri has prepared a decadent dessert for us." She smiled broadly at Pri, who was seated next to her.

Jeff hung back near the door connecting the kitchen. The

only empty seat at the table belonged to Curtis. Pri had stretched a piece of masking tape from his place setting to the back of his chair.

"We should make a space for you," I said, passing by Jeff, who was doing his best not to draw any attention in his direction.

"There are folding chairs in the basement," Penny said. I noticed the wine bottle she'd used to serve Curtis was resting next to her empty soup bowl.

"I'll help you," Pri offered, getting to her feet.

Penny started to protest, but Pri whispered something to her, which made her nod and return to her seat.

I needed to get the bottle without drawing any extra attention to what I was doing, so I gathered empty soup bowls and placed them on my tray. When I got to Penny's spot, I acted quickly.

"Could I borrow a napkin? I got soup on my hands."

"Of course." She handed me the napkin and her soup bowl.

I wiped my hands on the napkin. "Is this empty?" I lifted the wine bottle with the napkin, hoping I didn't look too obvious.

"Yeah, yeah. Feel free to take that." She didn't sound bothered. "The other empties are on the buffet, but just leave them. I'll get them later."

It was probably my imagination, but I felt like all eyes were on me as I skirted to the other side of the table to grab a few more bowls.

Pri followed me into the kitchen. I didn't know how it was possible, but it smelled even better than it had before. Liam had taken the pork loin out of the oven and was carefully slicing two-inch pieces of the savory roast.

"Don't touch these. I'm setting them over here," I said, to Pri, placing the bottle on the left side of the sink next to the silver tray Jeff had used to deliver soup.

Pri dragged her teeth over her bottom lip, taking slow cautious steps toward the sink. "Annie, I don't like the sound of that. Why are we sorting the dishes? What are you thinking? Are you thinking there's more at play here?"

"It's too soon to know yet, but I think that Curtis was murdered, and there's a small chance that there could be traces of poison in..." I didn't elaborate. Pri was smart enough to get my point.

"You think someone poisoned the wine?" She clasped her hand over her mouth. "Oh God. Penny poured the wine. Oh no. What are we going to do? We have to make sure the police don't think Penny did it. Patrick already accused her. Oh, this is bad."

"I know it's scary, but we're going to get through it together, okay?" I put my hand on her shoulder. "We have to make sure that we do everything by the book, for lack of a better phrase. That's the best way we can help Penny." I was being truthful, not only about needing to make sure we documented everything for the police but also about getting through this together. I'd already lost a best friend. Pri had been my steadfast supporter for years, and I was happy to be able to return the favor. Plus, one thing I learned unequivocally from Scarlet's death was the absolute need to document every detail. The police had botched evidence collection and failed to follow through on several leads. Now that the case had gone cold, it was much harder to track new leads.

My thoughts drifted to the research I'd been doing into the cold case my best friend Scarlet and I had been assigned in college. The case ultimately led to her death. Recently I'd discovered a chip in Professor Plum, my cat's collar. Scarlet had hidden the chip before she died. It contained photos and detailed notes about the murder of Natalie Thompson. It was the most information I'd had in years and had been a big break-through. The other thing that the files revealed was that the police had botched some of the evidence they gathered in inves-

tigating Natalie's disappearance. I wasn't going to let that
happen tonight.

"You know that she didn't do it," Pri said, glancing at me
and then looking at Liam to back her up. "We're talking about
Penny. When we walk through the orchard, she picks up worms
to move them off the path so they don't get squished. It's kind of
maddening because our power walks turn into strolls because
she has to stop every few feet to rescue another worm, but it's
also so endearing. Who saves worms? She would never hurt
anyone."

"Relax." I modeled slow breathing for her. "We don't think
Penny killed him either, but we have to be careful. We can't
make any assumptions at this point. We need to make sure that
we keep the crime scene as secure and pristine as possible."

Liam sprinkled fresh herbs on a juicy slice of the tender,
apple-chutney-filled pork. Thus far he'd been quiet; he was
clearly paying attention. "What do you know about Penny's
past? You haven't been dating for that long. Is there a chance
she could be hiding something from you?"

Pri gasped. "Hiding something? Like what? That's she a
secret serial killer?"

Liam shrugged. "I don't know."

Pri lunged forward. "Dude, I'll kill you for that."

I held her back.

"Don't come at me." Liam set the knife down and raised his
arms in a show of surrender. "I like Penny, but Annie's right; we
can't rule anyone out yet, and it's true that you've only been
dating for a few months. You do have to question why she
moved to Redwood Grove. Why buy this money pit? There are
tons of great properties in town."

"I swear to God, I'm about to murder you, Liam Donovan."
Pri set her jaw and gave me a hard, empty stare. "And to think
how many times I've defended you to Annie. You're talking
about my girlfriend. Penny is not a killer. End of discussion."

"All I'm saying is it's worth a little follow-up." He spooned herb potatoes onto the plate. "She and Curtis got into it. Maybe she had enough. I knew the guy from the pub. He had a way of getting under people's skin."

"Getting under Penny's skin and murder are not the same," Pri replied, throwing her arms across her chest in a protective stance.

"Agreed." He nodded, trying to appease her. I could tell that he was genuinely concerned from his gentle tone. "But before you go to war for this woman, you should make sure her background checks out. I like her, too, but you have to admit you don't know her that well."

Pri fumed. I could feel heat and rage radiating from her body.

"Let's take a beat," I said with a calmness I didn't feel. I wasn't used to playing referee between Liam and Pri. "We need to find a couple of extra chairs. I don't want Jeff sneaking out. I have my eye on him."

I hoped that shifting the conversation to Jeff, who was certainly high on my suspect list, would help de-escalate the tension. I wouldn't say this to Pri, but I agreed with Liam. Not that Penny was likely a killer, but there were some questions we needed to clear up, and we couldn't ignore the fact that she had the opportunity to tamper with Curtis's drink.

Pri gave Liam a parting glare. As we returned through the dining room, Penny flagged us down. "I forgot that I locked the basement door earlier. The keys are in the top desk drawer of the entryway. It's the big brass key. You can't miss it."

"We're on it," Pri assured her, dragging me into the hallway. "Listen, Annie, I take back everything I've ever said about Liam. He's an ass, and I'm sorry I ever tried to talk you into dating him. That's a best friend fail on my part."

"Pri, look. We're all stressed. Liam is trying to help." I sighed. I needed to come clean with her. "It's not only Liam. I suggested keeping the bottle for the police. I promise I don't think Penny's the killer, but like I said earlier the best way we can help her is to make sure that we follow proper protocol. Let's say we ditched the wine bottle for example, that would only lead the police to suspect her more."

She gasped, but I cut her off.

"You trust me. We've been friends for years. I don't think Penny did it, but we can't take any chances. Most likely, the police won't find anything in the bottle, and that will help rule Penny *out* as a suspect."

"Yeah, I get it. You're right." She opened the antique desk drawer and rummaged through it for the keys. Her face lost all its earlier heat as she lifted something out of the drawer and held a small vial filled with clear liquid for me to see. "Oh my God, Annie. What is this?"

EIGHT

"Annie, is this what I think it is? Is this a vial of poison?" She held it like it was a biohazard. "What's it doing here? Could this be what killed Curtis?" Pri's questions came fast and furious.

I tried to wrap my head around what I was seeing.

"Put it down," I cautioned.

"Holy crap. This can't be real. This can't be happening." Pri's voice was filled with panic as she held out her palm for me to take the vial. Her eyes ping-ponged around the entryway and to the living room. "Who put this here?"

"We have no idea what it is." I examined the vial, careful not to touch it. "But until we do know, you need to put it down."

"Because of fingerprints." Pri dropped the vial into the drawer like it was on fire. "Oh my God, am I implicated now?"

"No. I know it's hard but try to stay calm." I looked around for something to put the vial in. There was nothing. "Let's leave it in the drawer, go get the chairs, and then I'll discreetly come back for it."

Pri found the key and shut the vial in the drawer. "Holy hell, Annie, is Liam right? Am I dating a stone-cold killer? Am I the worst judge of character on the planet? Has Penny been using me? Has our entire relationship been a ploy?"

"Slow down." I patted her arm. "We don't know anything yet, including what's inside the vial. It could be perfume. Or it could be that someone is trying to set her up."

Pri threw her hands on her face. "I didn't think about that. Yes, that makes so much more sense. What if she's being set up? We have to help her."

Pri's range of emotions was dizzying. It made me realize how much she cared about Penny.

"Let's take things one step at a time." I tugged her away from the desk. "Right now, we need chairs."

"Annie, what would I do without you?" Pri leaned her head into my shoulder. "Thank you for being a voice of reason. I'm a mess. I'm barely functional, and like always, you're thinking rationally and methodically. I don't know how you do it."

"Don't worry, I'll totally break down later." I stuck out my tongue and made a funny face to try and break the tension. "I'm in crisis mode, but once it wears off, I'll be a sobbing, blubbering mess curled up on the floor." I rubbed her arm. "For now, we need to stick together and figure this out, okay?"

"That's good. I guess we can't all fall apart at the same time." She turned the key in the tiny keyhole cut into the vintage solid brass backplate.

I was impressed by how many of the original details Penny had preserved. The neo-classical knobs were probably worth a small fortune now with their egg and dart design.

"Be careful on the stairs," Pri cautioned, flipping on a yellowed bulb as old as the doorknobs. "Penny didn't have the budget to rebuild the stairs or do much to the basement, so it's a bit of a danger zone."

The floorboards sagged and creaked with each step. Exposed wood beams and unfinished rough flooring greeted us at the bottom of the stairwell. The basement hadn't been loved or restored like the main floors. It was a menagerie of old broken equipment, boxes, and supplies coated in years of dust and grime.

"It's creepy, isn't it?" Pri fumbled on the wall, dragging her hand until she found the light switch. To call the flickering bulb a light source was a stretch. A dim, muted glow lit our path. "I told Penny she needs to lock the basement not to keep people out but to keep the ghosts locked in."

I chuckled. "It's chilly." Frigid was a better word. The temperature dropped dramatically underground. A small leak dripped from one of the beams, and drops of water splattered on the floor in a rhythmic pattern. "Does Penny know about the leak?"

"I don't know." Pri shrugged. "I'll have to tell her about it. I wonder if there's a bucket over by the washing machine. Do you want to check while I get the chairs?"

"Sure." We parted ways. She went to a storage closet to our left, and I scanned the rickety shelving near the washer and dryer. Soap and organic dryer sheets were neatly stacked above the washer. A basket of clothes sat on top of the dryer. It could work in a pinch, but I didn't want to dump Penny's fresh laundry out.

I knelt to see if there was anything in the cupboard next to the washer. To my surprise, wet footprints led straight to the far wall. Someone had been down here. Recently. Was it Penny? Had she tossed in a load of laundry before the party started? But why would the floor be wet? And the prints didn't match her shoes. They were made from something sturdy—like a work boot.

Had her contractor been working in the basement earlier? Maybe she already knew about the leak. Every question that popped into my mind led to a new one. Like, why wouldn't

Penny or her contractor have placed a bucket or bowl under the beam to catch the drips?

In her lectures, Dr. Caldwell reinforced the importance of trusting our instincts. "If something feels off, it probably is. Never dismiss those feelings," she would say, pacing in front of the lecture hall with her glasses tucked on the bridge of her nose and a serious look on her narrow face. "Our intuition is tethered to our emotional intelligence. I'm not overstating things to say that your emotional intelligence may be your most important asset when you're out in the field. Refine it. Use it. You've accumulated a wealth of knowledge and experience in your coursework. Our subconscious minds are constantly drawing upon that knowledge base, making connections and noticing discrepancies that may not be immediately obvious. When we're referencing the idea of a 'gut feeling,' what we're actually noticing is our brain's incredible ability to analyze patterns based on our past experiences and expertise. If you take nothing else away from this class, take this piece of advice. Investigative work requires creativity to solve complex problems. Yes, of course, we need to follow procedures properly, but logic and analysis alone do not always provide a clear direction. Use your instincts to guide you."

Her words echoed in my head as I stared at the prints.

"Found them." The sound of Pri's voice made me jump.

"What is it? Why are you jumping? Spiders? Is it spiders?" Pri squealed, taking a step back. "Don't tell me it's spiders because I can't take creepy-crawlies right now."

"No, it's footprints. Look." I pointed to the prints.

Pri propped the folding chairs against the washer, bent closer and squinted. "That's weird. Is it my imagination, or do they appear as if they start at the wall?"

"They do." I was glad she confirmed what I already had been trying to wrap my head around. "The prints are pointed toward us like someone started at the wall and walked in this direction. Why? Or better the better question might be, how?"

"Where do they go after that?" Pri glanced behind us.

"There." I pointed to the fading prints that went from the wall to the base of the stairs.

Pri sucked air in through her nose in a giant gasp that made me nearly lose my balance. "It's a ghost, isn't it? There's no other explanation. People don't walk out of walls."

"I don't think ghosts wear wet boots," I said, standing and checking for anything else that seemed off. "Was Penny's contractor here earlier? Maybe he was doing work on the wall."

"Not that I know of." Pri stood, too, keeping her body close to mine like I was going to provide protection from our friendly basement ghost. "And even if he was, wouldn't the prints be pointing the opposite way?"

"Probably, but it could be that he was working on another leak in the wall, and his boots got wet in the process." It was a weak suggestion, but it was all I could come up with at the moment. The footprints felt important. That much I was sure of.

"Great. We have a massive storm, a dead body, a leaking basement, and a ghost. What else can go wrong tonight?" She threw her hands to her forehead and shook her head.

I didn't want to worry her more, and I needed time to let my brain process other possible explanations for the footprints. "Let's get the chairs upstairs," I suggested. "Dinner is probably ready to go, and I want to keep my eye on everyone until Dr. Caldwell arrives."

"Yeah, okay." Pri picked up a chair.

"Let's keep this to ourselves." I lifted the other chair and followed after her.

"What part?" she asked, sounding like she was on the edge of completely shutting down.

"All of it," I said solemnly. "At this point we don't know who we can trust."

Her head bobbed in agreement as we returned upstairs. My task list was quickly growing. I needed to get the vial, interview the other suspects, and cross my fingers and toes that Dr. Caldwell and her team would get here safely—and soon.

NINE

Liam was serving the last of the salads when we returned to the dining room. Pri set out a chair for Jeff next to Trishelle. He looked hesitant to sit next to her. Not that I blamed him. Trishelle seemed intent on taunting the young actor.

She dangled the fake, plastic spider in his face. "Welcome to my web, young chef. Eat at your own risk."

"That's in really poor taste," Penny said, scowling at Trishelle.

"Lighten up." She scoffed, rolling her eyes. "Everyone is so morbid. Be honest, did any of you even like the guy? I bet almost everyone at this table is relieved that he's dead." She flicked the spider, letting it land near her bare feet.

Jeff scooted his chair closer to the table. "Is this mine?" He motioned to a water glass.

"I haven't touched it," Trishelle replied with a slow grin.

Was she trying to make him uncomfortable?

"How is it out there?" Patrick asked Pri, brushing a crumb from his mobster jacket. "Any chance we can get out of here? Are the roads clear?"

"I don't know," Pri replied. "We didn't go outside."

"I'd like to remind you that no one can leave until the police arrive," I said, hoping my tone commanded authority.

"You've said that, but I'm not convinced that's correct," Patrick challenged, curling up the edges of his thin mustache with his thumbs and index fingers. "There's a guest list. Penny has our numbers and contact information. It seems like overkill to make us wait around, and quite frankly, how are you authorized to keep us here? You're not a police officer or detective."

How nice of him to state the obvious.

I wanted to shoot back a retort, but instead, I did my best to remain professional. "I understand why you might feel that way, but I assure you this is standard protocol. As we mentioned earlier, I have a degree and training in criminology. The police will need to take statements from each of us before they release us." I hated having to repeat myself. Patrick could take a lesson from Liam, who didn't seem to have any issue taking direction from me. I wondered if he would push back this much if a man were in charge. It was hard not to pick up on his sexist undertones.

"You're welcome to call them yourself," Pri added. "Dispatch was very clear that under no circumstances should anyone leave."

We'd already been over this. Why was Patrick pushing it again?

Could there be a reason he wanted to make an exit now?

Was he concerned that the police might find evidence on him?

I wanted to speak with him further, but in the short term, I had to get the vial before it potentially disappeared. Suddenly, I realized that someone was missing from the table. "Where's Ophelia?"

"She went to the bathroom," Patrick replied, motioning to the hallway with his thumb.

"We discussed staying together in pairs," I said, not able to conceal my irritation at this point. What was it with this group? My requests were simple—stay put, don't touch the crime scene, and stick together. Being temporarily in charge gave me a new appreciation for Dr. Caldwell. She made controlling a situation like this look so easy. I knew it wasn't, and I also knew that she had years of experience on me and the authority of a detective's badge.

Lately, I'd been giving much more consideration to the idea of returning to criminology, partly at Dr. Caldwell's urging and partly on my own accord. After assisting her with two previous cases and revisiting Scarlet's murder, I'd been feeling more drawn to stepping into the career path I once thought I was destined for.

But was this my path? Or was it something else?

Scarlet and I had intended to start our own private detective agency. When I thought about my future, I could see multiple paths—staying contentedly at the Secret Bookcase, going to work for Dr. Caldwell, or carving out my own way forward. For a long time, I couldn't even fathom the thought of striking out on my own. The detective agency had been Scarlet's vision. Joining the police force and training to be a full-fledged detective was Dr. Caldwell's vision. What was my vision? Was it this? Or was it time for me to seriously consider what the Annie Murray Detective Agency might look like?

I pushed the thought aside. "I'll go check on Ophelia. Everyone else, please stay in the dining room. The more we can adhere to these simple rules, the easier it will be for the police to conduct interviews once they arrive."

"I need my phone," Patrick said, setting down his wine glass. "If I'm going to be stuck here all night, I need to let my wife know."

That was a fair point. "Where is it?"

"In the study with the coats." Patrick stood. "I'll go with you now. You can babysit me since you're large and in charge."

I ignored his dig.

"What about my phone?" Trishelle asked, glancing around like she was checking to see who else was listening. "If we're not going to be entertained for dinner, I at least want my phone."

I acquiesced. If I wanted to keep everyone contained in one space, giving them access to their phones would hopefully appease them. "Okay, come with me. We'll do a phone run. Just give me one second." I hurried into the kitchen, grabbed a plastic bag for the vial, and tucked it into my bra.

Trishelle and Patrick were waiting for me at the entrance to the living room. Trishelle didn't bother to put her shoes on, and Patrick's energy made me wonder if he was going to try to make a break for it when we got to the front of the house. He shifted his weight from one foot to the other, like he was dancing to a silent disco.

The fire in the living room had nearly burned out. A few glowing embers cracked as we passed through the spacious room. "I'll wait for you to get your phones," I said, holding open the double glass doors to the study.

They went inside just as the power cut out. Everything was plunged into darkness. The only light I could see was the halo of copper emanating from the hearth.

Screams sounded in the dining room.

My stomach dropped.

It wasn't unexpected that we'd lost power, but I had been holding out hope that it would stay on. No light or electricity complicated an already tricky situation, but there was no time to sit around and worry about it. The good news was that we had already lit all of the candelabras in the dining room. Between those and the fireplace, we should be in good shape as long as everyone stayed put.

The bad news was losing power likely meant it was going to take even longer for the police to show up.

"I can't see anything," Trishelle yelled.

"I'm right here. Grab my arm," Patrick replied.

Another shriek sounded nearby. It was a high-pitched scream.

"Help. Help."

Ophelia.

She was probably stuck in a pitch-black bathroom.

"Hang on, I'm coming." I used the wall as my guide. Fortunately, I knew the layout of the farmhouse. The bathroom was two doors down on the right. The farther away I got from the dying embers of the fire, the harder it was to see.

I knocked on the bathroom door. "Ophelia, is that you? Are you okay?"

"Yes. It's me. The lights went out."

"I know. We lost power."

"This is straight out of the pages of *Macbeth*. I couldn't script a disaster of an evening like this if I tried."

I heard the sound of running water and her fumbling around.

"I'll help you back to the dining room. At least we have candles and a warm fire in there."

The door handle twisted twice. "It's stuck."

I tried on my side. The vintage handle clattered and clicked but didn't turn.

"I'm stuck." Her voice went up in pitch. "I don't do well in dark, tight spaces. Help me."

I jiggled the handle and used my hip to try and force the door open. It wouldn't budge, holding as steadfast as the deeply rooted trees in the orchard, standing strong in the fierce winds. "Hang on a sec, I'm going to get help."

"Hurry. I don't like this. I don't like it at all. This is eerily similar to *The Mousetrap*. I've directed a number of versions of the play. This is uncannily similar—we're trapped inside a guesthouse in inclement weather, and a murderer is among us. I'm not going to be the bait." She continued to shake the knob like a demanding toddler throwing a tantrum. "Get me out of here! Get me out of here—now."

"I'm trying. The handle is broken. I'm going to grab some tools, and I'll be right back," I promised.

I retraced my steps to the study using the fading candles as my light. I squinted, fumbling through the dark. Torrents of rain battered against the windows, casting creepy shadows on the ceiling. I gripped my candle tighter, my senses on high alert. "Did you find your phones?" I called to an empty room.

Where had they gone?

"Patrick, Trishelle, are you here?" I inched past the fireplace, stepping timidly so as not to trip over anything. I ran my hand along the elegant wallpaper, maintaining contact with the wall until I got closer to the entryway.

Was that the sound of the wind?

Why was I suddenly so cold?

I rubbed my shoulders, feeling the temperature drop as I rounded the corner and stepped into the entryway.

Sure enough, the front door was swung wide open, blowing in the rain, cold, and a smattering of leaves and debris. Fat raindrops pounded on the floorboards. Water pooled on the porch, creating tiny ripples and miniature streams that gushed down the steps.

"Trishelle, Patrick," I yelled over the howling wind.

Lightning cracked across the sky, briefly illuminating her silhouette. I startled and threw my hand over my chest as if that would protect me.

"I'm out here," Trishelle called from the porch. She used her turban to block the pelting rain.

I shielded my face from the lashing rain, unable to see anything other than the dark veil of mist. A deep, rumbling thunder growled in the distance. I couldn't tell how far away it was, but I didn't want to stick around to find out. "What are you doing out here?"

"Patrick is checking to see if the lines are down." Trishelle motioned to the blowing trees, their limbs bending like paper dolls from the screeching winds.

"Where is he?" I squinted to see in the darkness. Rain came down in sheets, obscuring the landscape. Everything was pitch black. It was futile. Patrick could be anywhere by now.

She clutched her turban with both hands, put it back on her head, and motioned with her neck. "He went that way, but it's so dark, I can't see him now."

"Go back inside," I said, thrusting my hand toward the door. Why had neither of them listened to me? I realized I wasn't officially a member of the Redwood Grove police department, but my orders had been clear.

"What about Patrick?" She stood on her toes and tried to peer around the edge of the porch. "He's still out there."

I couldn't believe she'd come outside barefoot. She had to be freezing.

"He's on his own. I told him not to leave." My first instinct about him had been right. The moment he had the opportunity, he had taken off. I didn't believe for a second the excuse that he was checking on the power lines. "Come on, we're letting the cold air rush in."

Trishelle didn't argue. She followed me back to the dining room, keeping one hand on her turban and leaving a trail of wet footprints behind her.

"I know this won't be a shocker, but it looks like the power's out, Annie," Pri said, holding a tealight under her chin that illuminated her face, giving it a mysterious glow. She stood at the head of the table near Penny like she was keeping watch on our unruly guests, waiting for someone else to attempt to break out of our sequestered dinner.

"It's out everywhere, and Ophelia is stuck in the bathroom. Keep an eye on everyone and don't let anyone leave."

She lifted the candle closer to her chin to amplify her

menacing presence. "I'll channel my inner Count Olaf. Don't worry, no one is getting out of here unnoticed on my watch."

I couldn't help but laugh. Pri was a huge fan of the Lemony Snicket novels and about as far away from the evil Count Olaf's personality as possible.

"Thanks." I shot her a smile and went straight to the kitchen.

Dozens of tealights lining the counters and island gave the space a cozy ambiance. The room was enveloped by a golden hue. Flames from burning clusters of candles in mismatched holders swayed in the air. It felt like I was walking into a proposal scene, short of having a dozen rose petals leading my path. Under other circumstances, it might have been romantic.

Annie, stop.

Why am I thinking about proposals now?

Liam garnished plates with sprigs of fresh herbs. "Hey, where you'd go? The dinner course is ready for service. I left the oven door open to let the heat out and it's a good thing that Pri's desserts don't need to be warmed up."

"Before you serve dinner, can I steal you for a minute?" Rosy light danced across his face, softening his angular jawline and causing my heart to skip a beat. "We have a guest stuck in the bathroom and I need your muscles."

"Thanks for noticing. As a matter of fact, I have been lifting at the gym." Liam flexed.

"You have such an inflated ego," I teased.

"When you have guns like this..." He trailed off and flexed both arms.

I rolled my eyes. "Just come help me."

"Okay, let me put the pork back in the oven so it doesn't get cold." He set the carving knife in the sink, placed trays of the pork tenderloin in the oven, and grabbed a Mason jar candle. "We have to see, right?"

I was glad for the candle and Liam's strong arms (not that I would ever tell him that) because the living room felt colder and darker, almost like Pri's ghost had escaped from the basement to haunt us.

"Anyone? Anyone? Help!" Ophelia banged on the bathroom door. "It's getting cold and claustrophobic in here."

Liam handed me the candle. "Hold this." He turned the knob and yanked with all of his strength. It broke off in his hand.

"Oh no." I positioned the candle so he could try to reattach the handle.

"Stop. Stop. What are you doing?" Ophelia sounded like a wild animal was attacking her.

"We're getting you out." Liam tossed the knob on the floor. It hit the hardwood with a thud. "Stand back."

"Are you breaking down the door? I don't know if that's a good idea." Ophelia sounded unsure.

I didn't blame her.

"On three. Here we go. One... two... three." He threw his shoulder into the door. It burst open.

"My hero." Ophelia swept forward like she was about to take a bow and collapsed in his arms. "Thank you. You saved me. I don't know how much longer I would have lasted in there."

"No problem." Liam reached down to pick up the knob. "We'll have to break it to Penny that I broke her door."

"I think she'll understand," I answered truthfully. A broken door handle was the least of her worries.

Ophelia's breath was shallow and labored like she was on the verge of hyperventilating. "Who did this to me?"

"Did what?" I asked, using the Mason jar like a flashlight to see into the small bathroom. Nothing seemed out of the ordinary. There was a pedestal sink, a towel rack, and floating shelves containing lotions and pretty soaps. I half expected to see someone lurking in the shadows, but there was nothing out of the ordinary.

"Locked me in the bathroom," she snapped, tossing her hands above her head and stomping her heavy combat boots on the floor.

"I think the handle is just old," I said, wondering why she was taking such a leap. Her boots also gave me a moment of pause. I noticed them earlier because I thought they were such an interesting fashion statement with her flowing cape and scarves. But my mind immediately went to the footprints in the basement. Could they match? Was Ophelia putting on an act? What if she'd been in the basement and then pretended to get locked in the bathroom as an alibi?

"The handle isn't old. Someone locked me in. I heard them do it." She brushed past me. "Someone is out to kill me."

TEN

Ophelia's glowering eyes reminded me of an angry cat. She tossed her purple cape over her shoulder and fumed. "I don't know why you two are just standing there. We need to confront the culprit. Someone tried to kill me."

"Kill you?" I questioned out loud. How had she gone from getting stuck in a bathroom to murder so quickly? "I'm not sure how I follow. How would they have killed you by locking you in the bathroom?"

"Isn't it obvious?" She scoffed, wrapping her cape tighter around her shoulders like a security blanket.

"No." What was I missing? She couldn't be serious.

"The inhumanity of it all." Ophelia huffed. "Imagine being locked in a cold, dark bathroom all night knowing that there's a crazed killer on the loose just waiting for the right moment to strike. I don't want to begin to imagine what could have happened."

Liam stifled a laugh as he put the knob in his apron pocket.

I caught his eye. We shared a chuckle as Ophelia stomped back to the dining room, her heavy black combat boots thudding against the wood floors.

"The *inhumanity*?" Liam couldn't contain his grin.

This moment of levity was exactly what I needed. I was glad to have Liam on the same page. If you had asked me that a few months ago, I would have shrugged off the idea, but I was struck by how much more we had in common than I originally thought and that we seemed to share the same slant and perspective on the absurd dramatics of the group.

"I mean, she might have had to wrap herself in a towel to keep warm." I said, pretending to wrap my arms around my shoulders.

"Or make a pillow out of toilet paper?" Liam's eyes twinkled mischievously. "How could she survive? It's impossible."

A wave of much-needed calmness washed over me as we connected over Ophelia's disingenuous response to being stuck in the bathroom for what couldn't have been more than ten or fifteen minutes.

"Has anyone ever told you that your eyes are like emeralds when you smile?" Liam asked, leaning slightly closer to me.

I caught a faint whiff of grilled onions and garlic on his skin. The momentary calmness vanished as he held my gaze, staring into my eyes like he could see through me. My heart pounded against my chest, rattling like the breeze in the trees outside.

Keep it together, Annie.

Why did my knees feel like they were about to collapse?

And why did my body betray me this easily?

I wanted to sink into him and let the awfulness of the night vanish in his arms.

My throat seized. I forced a swallow and tugged on my necklace, not knowing how to respond. "Thanks," I managed to squeak out.

He brushed a strand of wavy hair from his eyes and cleared his throat.

Is he about to kiss me?

Here?

Now?

My heart pounded so loudly that I was fairly sure everyone in the dining room could hear it, but surprisingly, I didn't care. I wanted this. I wanted Liam's lips on mine. Would they be soft or slightly rough?

"Annie." His voice caught, deepening with a new tenderness.

After all our back-and-forth banter and debates, I couldn't believe our first kiss was going to happen now. Curtis was dead, the guests were restless, Patrick had taken off, and Ophelia claimed to have been intentionally locked in the bathroom. For the briefest flash, I didn't care.

I stood on my toes, feeling wobbly and off-center.

Liam caressed my cheek with his thumb. "Annie, you're so gorgeous, clever, ridiculously smart, bookish, and you make me crazy in the best possible way. I think you know that I'm into you, but I want to make sure you feel the same."

His profession of his feelings for me was right on par for Liam. Was he complimenting me? Or was he also slightly insulting me?

"Bookish?" I raised my brows and tried my best to stay balanced. Why did he have to be so tall?

"Bookish in a good way." He cupped my face in his hands.

"Don't backtrack," I said, meeting his eyes. "I believe you were trying to sweep me off my feet?"

He sighed. "Am I failing miserably?"

"Not at all." I put my hand over his thumb to keep it pressed against my skin. My cheeks smoldered like the embers in the hearth. "This is our thing."

I was about to kiss him when the sound of police sirens interrupted us.

"Damn." Liam pulled away and shook his head. "Is the universe conspiring against us?"

I felt the same way, but maybe it was better. If Liam and I

were seriously going to take our friendship—or whatever this was—to the next level, it was probably a good idea to proceed slowly with a bit more caution. I needed to talk this through with Pri. Although since she was furious with Liam for considering Penny as a potential suspect, she might not be quite as enthusiastic about the idea of us dating.

"This isn't over, Murray. I'm taking you out for a real date, dinner, drinks—"

"Dancing?" I interrupted him with a goofy grin, trying to picture Liam on the dance floor.

"If that's what it takes to win your heart, sign me up—ballroom, line dancing, salsa."

I punched him playfully in the arm. "Dinner and a drink would be nice."

"Good, because no excuses, it's happening." Liam walked to the front door with one last longing glance.

The sirens grew louder as blue, red, and white lights danced off the windows. The cavalry had arrived.

My shoulders and jaw loosened as Liam propped the door open for the police. Everything shifted almost instantaneously.

Dr. Caldwell led the charge.

A sudden lightness flooded through me. I let out a huge breath and smiled at her in relief as she walked toward us.

She was dressed for the weather in a pair of black slacks, stylish yellow ankle rainboots, and a matching tailored, waterproof yellow jacket. She was petite with short white hair and thick black glasses.

"Annie, excellent. I was comforted to hear that you were on the scene. I'm sorry it's taken us so long. Fill me in. What do you know? What do I need to know?" She didn't hesitate or take time for small talk.

"Should I continue with dinner service?" Liam asked, motioning toward the kitchen. "Without power, I'm concerned everything will get cold, but obviously it's up to you."

"Go ahead," Dr. Caldwell replied with a curt nod. "I'll come find you for your statement shortly."

I felt like I was back in school and had been caught cheating on a test, not that I would ever have considered cheating. Dr. Caldwell was so astute that I wondered if she picked up on the charged energy between me and Liam.

"Shall we have a seat?" She removed a black leather notebook from her satchel and motioned to the collection of couches in front of the fireplace.

Her team tromped into the entryway with bright flashlights, first aid kits, and battery-powered lanterns.

"Secure the dining room and check on the deceased," Dr. Caldwell directed them. "I'll be with you momentarily."

"We moved the body," I admitted, taking a seat on the edge of the couch.

Dr. Caldwell set one of the lanterns on the coffee table. It provided a generous amount of light. Her face remained passive, but I noticed the fine creases lining her eyes deepened. "You moved the body?"

"He died in the dining room. We weren't sure how long it was going to take for you to get here with the storm, so Liam and I moved him into the pantry. We used gloves and made sure to secure his place setting as well as compile the dishes that were used to serve him."

She made a note. "Okay, fine. Walk me through what happened."

I let out a slow breath and composed myself. "I went through the steps you taught me. Although I do have new appreciation for how challenging it can be to keep the suspects in one place. The first thing I did was create a timeline. It's in the kitchen. I can share it with you if it would be helpful."

"Absolutely. I'm impressed, although not at all surprised." She smiled. "Let's start with the big picture."

I told her about the events leading up to dinner, Curtis's death, and everything I'd learned in the aftermath.

"Excellent work, Annie. Truly. This is most helpful." She pulled in a breath and gave me a curt nod.

"There are a few more things I should tell you before you start to take witness statements." I glanced behind us to make sure we were still alone.

"Please, continue." She waved her pencil to encourage me.

"When Pri and I went to the basement to get chairs, I noticed a set of wet footprints. They appeared to be going from the stairs to the washing machine and then dead-ending at an outside wall. I haven't come up with an explanation or connection to Curtis's death, but they struck me as strange at the time and I know from your teachings how important it is not to dismiss something that feels off."

She bobbed her head in acknowledgment. "I'm glad that lesson stuck. I'll be sure to have my team take a look."

"You'll need to check with Penny to confirm this, but it doesn't sound like anyone was downstairs. I've been wondering if perhaps Curtis was snooping around before dinner. He was trying to buy the property, so maybe he was looking for old paperwork. I'm not sure. Like I said, I haven't come up with a firm theory yet."

"Take a minute." She rested her pen on her notebook. "Let's talk it through. Why don't you give me your initial impressions of each of the suspects."

I appreciated this about her as a professor and now as a mentor. She never rushed a conversation or attempted to direct the narrative. She made space for ideas to sift and flow.

"The one thing I know for sure is that whoever was in the basement had wet boots. It could have been Curtis. Ophelia is also wearing boots. She got locked in the bathroom and is convinced that someone tried to trap her inside. I don't believe that story. She's naturally dramatic. She was also furious with Curtis before dinner because he interrupted their warmups."

"Interesting." Dr. Caldwell tapped the paper with the tip of her pen. "How would the killer have benefited from locking her in the bathroom?"

"Exactly." I rubbed my hands together to keep my fingertips from going numb. Without power, the temperature inside was dropping quickly. "Unless it was a ruse. We made it clear that everyone needed to stay together in the dining room. Ophelia left while Pri and I were in the basement. Maybe she went looking for something—evidence she left behind?"

Dr. Caldwell made a note. "Mm-hmm."

"Trishelle is on my suspect list. I'm not clear on her connection to Penny or the estate. She briefly referenced growing up in Redwood Grove. She got out of her chair shortly before Curtis began exhibiting breathing issues. The actor playing the victim found a fake spider in her drink. I don't know if she put it in her wine or if someone else did to keep attention off them while they slipped poison into Curtis's glass, but during the commotion, wine spilled on Trishelle's dress, and she went to the buffet to get a napkin. The problem is that I wasn't expecting Curtis to die, so I wasn't paying close attention to any of the suspects at that point. I was waiting for the fake murder to take place."

"It's understandable. Any observations are helpful, as you know," Dr. Caldwell said, encouraging me to continue. "I'm making a note to run background checks on everyone."

"Jeff, the young actor playing the chef, had access to the kitchen and everyone's food and drink. He served Curtis the soup. That's the last thing Curtis ate. My best description of him is that he's skittish. He's very nervous. There could be an innocent reason, like nerves from performing and having to do improv with the guests, but I don't think we can rule him out either. Curtis was awful to him while they were warming up. There's definitely bad blood between them."

"Bad blood. Is that a technical term?" Dr. Caldwell tipped her glasses on the bridge of her nose.

"That was a term in our textbooks, wasn't it?" I smiled. "Fine, maybe not. Lastly, there's Patrick. He's high up on my list right now because he completely ignored me and took off in the middle of the storm. I have no idea where he is. I accompanied him and Trishelle to the study to get their phones. When the power went out, he ran outside, supposedly to check on the power lines, but I haven't seen him since. He's a real estate developer eager to raze Curtis's farm and pave the way for single-family homes. He's made Penny an offer, too. Money is a solid motive. He stands to gain the most financially from Curtis's death."

"Pause that thought." She held up a finger. "Hang tight for a minute. I'm going to task one of my team to conduct a search of the grounds immediately."

I waited for her to call to one of her officers and direct them to look for Patrick before she returned to questioning me.

"Tell me more about Penny." She flipped through her notes. "You mentioned when we first began speaking that Penny poured Curtis's wine."

I didn't like Dr. Caldwell's tone, although I knew she was only doing her due diligence. "That's right. I don't think it could be her. I don't want it to be her. We've become friends, and she's dating Pri."

She held up a finger. "I hope I know the next thing you're going to say."

"Yeah. I can't let my personal biases influence the investigation. It's true that she served him; she was angry with him, and Pri and I found a vial in the desk near the front door."

"A vial?" Dr. Caldwell craned her neck in the direction of the entryway.

"I'll show you." I removed the Ziploc from my bra. "I was going to grab it and put it with the other evidence, but then when everything went dark, it was chaos. I have no idea what's in the vial. It could be nothing or something benign."

"Let's have a look." Dr. Caldwell took off her rain jacket and left it on a chair.

I walked to the desk and opened the drawer, but to my shock, the vial was gone. "It's not here," I said to Dr. Caldwell. "Someone's taken it."

ELEVEN

I searched the contents of the drawer again, hoping that when Pri and I had opened it last, the vial had rolled to the back. It hadn't. There was no sign of the little glass container. "It was here before we went downstairs," I said to Dr. Caldwell.

She pursed her lips together and frowned. "I don't doubt that it was. I'll have one of my team sweep the desk for prints and follow up on everything you've shared. I do appreciate your insight, Annie. It's all the more reason to remind you that you have a job waiting should you decide you want it."

"Thank you. I appreciate it." I wasn't ready to give her a solid yes. Not yet. Tonight was good practice at what running my own investigation might be like and I was too close to the situation at the present moment to be able to have any clarity or insight. Plus, I had the Secret Bookcase and Hal to consider and Scarlet's murder case lingered in the back of my head.

I was glad that Dr. Caldwell never pressured me.

I knew that sooner or later I was going to have to give her a definitive answer, but for the time being I was happy just to know that her offer was still out there.

"I'm going to speak with the dinner guests and check in

with my team. I would love to see your timeline. If you can jot down any additional notes or observations, I'll take whatever you have to give me." She picked up her flashlight and waited for me to stand.

"Of course."

"If it's not too much to ask, I'd love to have you consult on this case. You've been on the scene and can provide a unique slant."

"I'd be happy to," I replied truthfully, feeling a happy flush return. If she had asked me to stay out of her way, I would have been devastated. I was invested in figuring out who had killed Curtis and would do anything I could to help clear Penny from Dr. Caldwell's suspect list.

"Excellent. Let's touch base after I finish taking statements."

She went to the dining room. I stared at the drawer before giving it one last check. My fingers fumbled through brochures, keys, rubber bands, tape, and a stack of junk mail. The vial was gone.

My mind raced, searching for answers as I shut the drawer. Someone must have taken it between the time Pri and I went downstairs and when Dr. Caldwell and the police showed up. Assuming no one other than Ophelia left the dining room, that gave me three suspects—Ophelia, Patrick, and Trishelle.

An almost ghostly draft seeped through the narrow gap beneath the front door. I rubbed my shoulders to stave off the chill. Ophelia could have taken the vial before locking herself in the bathroom, and both Patrick and Trishelle had been out of my sight long enough to grab the vial without being seen.

Could Patrick have swiped it before he made his escape outside? Or could Trishelle have gotten into the drawer after he left?

If the vial contained the poison that killed Curtis, it was possible that the killer had stashed it in the desk, knowing that their fingerprints were on the container. They could have planned to retrieve it at the end of the evening on their way out the door without anyone being the wiser. I hadn't been convinced that the vial was important, but now that it was missing, it was impossible to deny a connection.

I shuddered as the draft brushed against my skin like I was being tickled with a feather. I knew it was the wind, but the cold pierced through me like a shard of ice. Or maybe it was that the reality of Curtis's murder was starting to soak in.

I needed more information.

I needed to focus on facts.

For instance, what substance had killed Curtis? What was the window of time in which he had ingested the poison? How long did it take to have an effect on him? If it was a fast-acting drug, then everyone in the dining room was a suspect. However, if the toxin took hours or days to release, it could open an entirely new pool of suspects.

I sighed, wishing I had the answers now.

These were all questions that would have to be answered by a team of experts. Until Dr. Caldwell received the autopsy and toxicology reports, we were only making assumptions. And unlike in the movies, the reports could take a while to come back.

There wasn't much I could do, so I returned to the kitchen to get my timeline and write down everything else while it was still fresh. The police had broken off into each corner of the dining room to interview guests separately.

"Hey, Annie," Liam greeted me as he gathered used dishes and placed them in the sink. "There's no hot water and the dishwasher isn't functional without power, so I don't know what I'm doing. Just stacking stuff aimlessly and staying on dish-watch, I guess. The police told me to make sure that no one touches that stack." He gestured to Curtis's dishes and the other things we'd set aside.

"I've heard dish-watch is the dream surveillance gig," I teased, trying to catch his eye.

He must not have noticed my attempt to flirt because his gaze remained glued to the dishes. "What did Dr. Caldwell say?"

Is he not interested?

Does he regret that we almost kissed?

I tried to silence the nagging worries taking root.

"Well, what did she say?" he repeated, his eyes still studying the dishes as if they might take a page from *Beauty and the Beast* and suddenly animate and dance out of the kitchen.

It was back to business between us, like we hadn't nearly kissed minutes ago.

If Liam was going to pretend it hadn't happened, I guessed I would, too.

"She just asked me a bunch of questions. I told her I would share my notes and the timeline we put together." I wanted to ask him if something was wrong (I mean, aside from the obvious), but I knew Dr. Caldwell would be ready for me soon and I wanted to make sure I added in everything else I'd observed.

I grabbed the notebook and made space on the island, moving one of the tapered candles closer so that I could see while I updated my thoughts. It was strange and somehow fitting to be writing by candlelight. This was how the Wentworth family would have shared meals and cooked. It gave me a new appreciation for modern technology and a longing for simpler times. I could picture Liam and me chopping vegetables grown fresh in our garden with the ambiance of flittering candles and the sound of rain splatting against the windows a century ago.

My cozy daydream was interrupted by two uniformed officers who entered the dining room with a purpose. "We're going to need you to vacate this room while we prepare the body for transport."

I gulped. How had I forgotten, even for a second, that Curtis's body was merely feet away from me in the pantry?

I grabbed the notebook and scooted out of the way as they maneuvered a gurney through the tight space.

"We don't want to watch them load the body, do we, Murray?" Liam asked rhetorically under his breath, holding the door open for me and practically pushing me out of the room.

"Nah, I've seen enough death tonight." I backed away toward the dining room.

"Me too. Murder wasn't supposed to be on the menu." Liam shuddered slightly. It was the first time I'd seen any indication that he was physically rattled. "I'm sorry this happened, Annie, I..." He struggled to find the right words and then trailed off. His mouth opened again but it formed no words as he gave me a slow, disbelieving headshake.

I was glad to see even a tiny chink in his armor. Not that I wanted him to be in distress, but he was so skilled at holding it together and appearing unfazed. It was good to see that he wasn't immune to the after-effects of witnessing a violent crime.

Pri reached for my arm when I entered the dining room. "I've been dying to talk to you. You already spoke with Dr. Caldwell, right?" Her hair spilled out from her ponytail. She gnawed on her fingernail like she was devouring corn on the cob. "I'm so worried about Penny. Dr. Caldwell has been talking to her this entire time. It doesn't look good. What if she arrests her?"

I pulled her hand away from her face and squeezed it in a show of solidarity. "Pri, it's going to be okay." I hated seeing her so wound up. Pri was usually the life of the party and eternally optimistic. "You know how professional Dr. Caldwell is. She's not going to jump to any conclusions or make an arrest before she has all the facts. This is normal. It's exactly what's supposed to happen after a suspicious death, and she's likely focused on Penny since this is Penny's house and party."

"What about the vial? Did you get it?" Pri's voice was so low I had to strain to hear her.

"It's gone," I whispered back, checking around to make sure we didn't have listening ears nearby. No one was paying attention to us. Everyone stuck to themselves, nibbling on bites of the decadent dark chocolate pudding and berry tarts. The tone was subdued and serious. Understandably so. The presence of Dr. Caldwell and her team made the reality that this was a homicide investigation that much more real.

"Gone. What? How? Oh, God, Annie. That's terrible. That's going to be super bad for Penny, don't you think?" Pri bit her bottom lip and shook her head so hard that it made my neck hurt.

I started to respond.

"No, wait. It's not." She cut me off before I could reply. "This is good news. This is really good news. Penny couldn't have taken the vial because she's been here in the dining room the entire time. She never left. Everyone at dinner will vouch for her." Pri whistled with relief.

I didn't want to mention that we couldn't be sure that was true. Penny could have left the dining room while we were in the basement, but there was no reason to bring it up now. I needed Pri to be as level-headed as possible if we were going to figure out who had killed Curtis.

"What do you know about Patrick?" I asked, dropping the subject.

"You think he did it?" Pri sounded relieved. She let go of my hand and fixed her ponytail. "I don't like him. I haven't since the first time I met him. He came by one day early on when Penny and I were tearing down the old wood paneling. He made her an offer on the spot—a low offer, by the way—and when she told him she wasn't interested, he insulted her, basically implying that as a woman in her early thirties, she has no business savvy and that he would be doing her a favor by taking the orchard and farm off her hands."

"I got that vibe from him for sure." Patrick came across as someone who liked to be the most important and knowledgeable person in the room, and his antiquated ideas about women in business left nothing to the imagination.

"He did the same with Curtis, but it sounds like he was even more forceful." I kept the notebook tucked under my arm. I wanted to take notes but didn't want to look obvious to the other guests. No one else needed to know that I was working with Dr. Caldwell. It would be better that way.

"Yep." Pri ran her finger along the dagger temporary tattoo on her forearm. She had designed it specially for the occasion with a bouquet of red roses bursting from the tip of the blade. Her artwork had a signature whimsical flair with little flourishes and tiny scattered rose petals surrounding knife-like confetti. "Like Penny mentioned earlier, he was interested in the farm and orchard, but Curtis's property was his ultimate goal. He was desperate to get Curtis's land. It had the best potential for development. I don't understand the zoning, but the Wentworth farm would need a lot more grading and work done to get it level. Curtis's land is apparently much more desirable, but Curtis refused, repeatedly. Patrick was angry. He wouldn't take no for an answer. Penny told me that he was at Curtis's farm almost every day. He kept showing up. I guess he figured that the squeaky wheel eventually gets the grease, but his pressure tactics didn't work."

"Which could mean that his failed attempts to convince Curtis to sell forced his hand, and he decided to try another tactic." I tapped my finger to my chin, considering the possibilities.

"There was no way Curtis was ever going to sell to Patrick." Pri scowled and twisted her lips together. "Not a chance. The only way Patrick was going to get that land was if Curtis was dead."

We both grew quiet, thinking of the implications.

"Do you have any sense of what the property is valued at?"

"No." Pri glanced to the far end of the room where Dr. Caldwell was still questioning Penny. "Penny will know. She got this for a steal, but only because the house was in such bad shape. I don't think Curtis has done much work on his property either, but he must have been making a decent income from the farm because, as you know, he wanted to buy the vineyard from Penny and expand his offering."

The more I considered it, the more I was leaning toward Patrick as the most likely suspect. With Curtis out of the way, his estate would likely go up for sale, and Patrick would be first in line to make an offer. It explained his behavior. Why else would he run? Getting his phone was likely a distraction. He might have been planning to make a run for it anyway and then the power going out gave him the perfect chance.

If he poisoned Curtis, he could have stashed the vial in the desk and grabbed it on his way out the door. I tried to recall whether they'd had any interactions during dinner. The problem I kept bumping into was that the two men had been seated as far away from one another as possible.

How could he have slipped the poison into Curtis's food or drink?

Or could he have used a drug that took longer to interact? Perhaps he poisoned Curtis before we'd even begun the appetizer course.

A knock thudded in the other room.

Dr. Caldwell tore her eyes away from Penny and turned in the direction of the sound.

The banging continued.

She caught my eye and signaled me to come closer.

"Hang on," I said to Pri.

Dr. Caldwell gestured to the front of the house. "Annie, would you mind seeing who's here? The door should be unlocked."

"No problem." I hurried to the front. The door was indeed unlocked, but the knocking continued. I opened it to find two construction crew members dressed in bright yellow, reflective raingear standing on the porch.

"Evening, miss. We're here to let you know that you have downed lines that we're going to repair, but we will need to access the grounds. Are you okay with that?"

"I'm not the owner, but I'm sure that she'll be just fine with that." I knew I didn't need to check with Penny to give them permission to do whatever was needed to get the power running again as well as inform Dr. Caldwell the crew was going to be on the property.

"Good. We'll go ahead and get started. There's one more thing. We noticed the emergency vehicles. No one came in contact with the downed lines, did they?"

"No. We're having a dinner party, and one of the guests had a medical emergency."

The electrical worker nodded with understanding. "Got it. Okay, we'll proceed as planned, then."

I thanked them profusely. It was incredible that they were willing to work in the middle of the storm. "Please come get food when you're done. We have plenty of leftovers and a warm fire."

As I shut the door I noticed movement out of the corner of my eye. I turned around just in time to see Patrick standing at the top of the basement stairs.

TWELVE

"What are you doing?" I asked, not caring that my tone sounded accusatory. How had he gotten into the basement? And why was he downstairs?

"I was checking to see if a breaker blew." He yanked the basement door closed behind him. His retro suit was soaked. It looked like he had taken a plunge into the Pacific Ocean. Water pooled at his feet and dripped from his forehead. He fiddled with his mustache, which reminded me of a soggy spaghetti noodle.

"You've been gone for at least a half hour."

"So? At least I'm trying to help." He folded his arms behind his back. "Everyone else around here is content to sit back and do nothing like we're all helpless fools. We're not. I'm a man of action. I know your generation doesn't want to take any advice, but what you need to understand is if you listen every once in a while, you might actually learn something. I'm tired of the attitude that you have to wait for a hero to sweep in. Be your own god-damn hero."

Why the sudden impassioned speech?

Was he hiding something?

"You're going to have to give me more than that." I planted my feet firmly, making my stance as wide as possible to match his energy. "Trishelle told me you went outside to see if there were any downed power lines."

Patrick kept his hands secured behind him. "That's right. Someone had to do something. Everyone else is fine sitting around like prisoners, not me. As a real estate developer, I have a general understanding of electrical and plumbing. I walked the perimeter to see if I could spot a downed line so we could call it in. When I didn't find anything outside, I went to the basement to check the breakers."

I couldn't understand how having knowledge of electrical and plumbing would qualify him to do anything with the power lines. Also, his timing didn't add up. Nor did the fact that he claimed not to find any downed lines outside. The crew just told me they'd found the problematic lines. Not to mention, there was no need to pinpoint the spot of the power outage before calling it in.

He used his left hand to wipe water from his brow, leaving his right hand behind his back and stealing a gaze toward the front yard. "Did I hear that the power company is here now?"

"Yes. They've found the problem and are getting started on repairs now."

"Good." Patrick stuffed something into the back of his pants. Then he rolled up the sleeve of his drenched retro suit jacket and tapped on the oversized gold watch secured to his wrist. "Excellent. That means we can leave. My wife is worried sick about me, and I'm done playing murder with a bunch of strangers. This was supposed to be an evening of networking for me, and instead, it's turned into a ridiculous farce."

"I'm afraid you can't just leave. You'll need to speak with Dr. Caldwell or one of her police officers. They're in the dining room taking statements now." My muscles tightened in readiness. There was no way I was going to let him out of my sight before Dr. Caldwell had a chance to question him.

He coughed and pounded on his chest like he'd swallowed wrong. Was that his tell?

In my training, we'd learned how to pay attention to subconscious behavior or reactions that might indicate deception or nervousness—sweating, changes in breathing patterns, microexpressions.

Patrick was harder for me to read. Maybe it was because of his costume choice—the mobster pinstriped suit made it challenging not to peg him as shady. His biased and outdated ideas about women and inclination to want to lecture me about business only added to his persona.

The question was, was it a persona?

Was this how Patrick acted in normal business exchanges or was he stepping into character tonight?

I had to keep him talking, and in order to do that, I needed to remain as composed as possible and come up with an angle that would make him more likely to open up to me. I racked my brain for what that could be.

"The police are here?" he asked, clearing his throat.

"Yeah, and I have to tell you that it doesn't look good for you." He had given me the perfect opportunity. "They know you left despite explicit orders not to do so."

He used his drenched jacket sleeve to try and soak up the water. It was futile.

"You're probably one of the top suspects," I continued. "You have the most to gain financially now that Curtis is dead. It's no secret that you were trying to buy him out. With him gone, you have a clear and direct path to easily purchasing his property."

"Wait, wait, wait. I don't like the sound of this." He rubbed his hand down his wet pant legs and then scraped his hand through his hair. "That's not what happened."

"Do you want to explain what did happen?" My acute

sense of purpose came into focus. I recognized that he was nervous. He couldn't fake it any longer.

"Can I at least get a towel?" His eyes didn't blink. He pinched his lips tight to keep them from trembling. "I'm going to become hypothermic soon. Some thanks I get for trying to be a team player and help out. I could have stayed inside in the comfort of the dining room drinking my wine, but I risked my life for everyone."

"There are towels in the bathroom." I motioned toward the living room, keeping my stance firm to show that I wasn't going to budge.

"Let me dry off, and then I'll tell you what I know." He pasted on a smile, his mustache curling over his lip like a cartoon villain. "I get that you're tight with the detective, and I have information that they're going to want to hear, but first, let me at least try to dry off."

"Go ahead." I waited for him.

"No, ladies first, I insist." Patrick gave me a slight bow.

I didn't buy his act of chivalry at all. He wanted me to go first because he didn't want me to see whatever he was hiding behind his back. That was fine; I would play along if there was a chance he was going to share anything of value.

I stood guard in front of the bathroom. I wasn't going to give him an inch.

He emerged after a few minutes with his hair ruffled and a soggy towel draped over his shoulders. "Okay, listen, here's the truth. Yes, I made multiple offers on Curtis's property. Offers that he was downright idiotic to refuse, but I didn't kill him."

"I'm not sure that's new information." I laced my fingers together and continued to hold firm. Patrick was the kind of guy who was used to people, especially women, ceding their power to him, I needed to make it clear that wouldn't be happening with me.

"I didn't have to kill him to take possession of the farm

because it's already in foreclosure," Patrick said, smoothing down his damp hair. "I'm working with the bank on finalizing the details now. The bank owns the property. I've made them an offer that they're very pleased with, as am I. Come next week, I'll be the sole owner of Curtis's farmhouse and land. Why would I kill him when I already own him?" He lifted his chin and gave me a frozen smile.

I had to give him credit. This was new information. Curtis had been foreclosed on. Why would he be trying to buy a section of Penny's land? Was it because he knew that the fore-closure sale was going to go through, and he needed somewhere else to live? But that didn't make sense. How would he have the cash to make a purchase? And there weren't any livable struc-tures in the grape fields.

"You can confirm all of this with the bank. What am I saying? Not you—the police." Patrick used the towel to dab his neck. He must have secured whatever he'd been hiding behind his back while he was drying off in the bathroom.

"You'll need to share this with Dr. Caldwell," I said, trying to make sense of Curtis's motives for wanting Penny's land.

"Fine. Bring me to her. What are we waiting for? The sooner we get this over with, the sooner I'm out of here. I've got nothing to hide." He held out the towel as if to show me there was nothing behind his back.

I wasn't sure that was true. Patrick was hiding something, but I believed he was telling the truth about the foreclosure. There wasn't much more I could do about it until Dr. Caldwell had a chance to verify his statement with the bank.

What was more curious were the inconsistencies in his behavior. When our conversation turned to more incriminating topics, Patrick suddenly lost some of his bravado. That was a red flag.

"You know you really should be focusing your attention

elsewhere. I don't know why you're bothering with me." He tossed the towel on the bathroom floor.

"What do you mean?"

"Ophelia is the one who I'd be keeping my eye on if I were you." He tapped the side of his eye twice.

I frowned. "Why do you say that?"

"You don't know?" Patrick folded his neck and bent his head forward like a turtle peeking out of its shell.

"Know what?"

"Curtis pulled every last cent of his funding from the Redwood Curtain Players. Curtis was one of their largest donors, if not the largest. Without his money, the theater group is going to have to close. They're not even slightly profitable. They barely cover basic operating costs. Losing Curtis's annual donation is most likely going to force them to shutter their doors permanently." He sounded almost proud that he was divulging this information, as if he was taking pleasure in the theater's impending closure.

"How do you know this?"

"Because Ophelia approached me about taking on the role of lead sponsor. She has big ideas for future growth, and I have to credit her; she put together a solid pitch about how important having a thriving arts community would be when it comes to attracting new residents." He tossed the towel over his shoulder. "I've been considering it. It could be good PR optics for my business. New home buyers always like to feel like builders are part of the community. It could be a good match. I throw her a little cash to keep the lights on and, in return, garner positive press and community goodwill."

"I'm not sure I follow your logic. If she lost Curtis's funding but knew that you were going to step in and donate to the theater group, why would she kill him?"

"Oh, because the woman is unhinged and completely unstable." Patrick smirked with an unnatural stiffness. "You've met her, yes? Have you been paying attention to her outlandish behavior? It's too dramatic for the stage. She took the news that Curtis was withdrawing his annual donation as if it were a personal assault. She went on a rampage. I can't believe everyone in Redwood Grove isn't talking about it. I happened to be there that day, and it was ugly. I've never seen anyone lose control like that."

I did agree with him that Ophelia liked the spotlight and certainly leaned into her dramatic side.

"I'm telling you, watch out for that woman. If she has a personal vendetta against you, like she did with Curtis, then your fate is in her hands." He sauntered toward the dining room, notably not insisting that I go in front of him this time.

Was his earlier show of chivalry because he was hiding whatever had been behind his back? Whatever it was couldn't have been that big—perhaps the size of a small vial?

I scanned the bathroom just in case Patrick had stashed something in the shower or cabinet.

No luck.

There was nothing other than some soggy towels and pretty hand soaps.

I let out a long breath.

Finding an item would have been thrilling, but I was undeterred.

Our conversation had been illuminating. Curtis was about to be foreclosed, Patrick already owned the property, and Ophelia was furious that Curtis had canceled his donation to the Redwood Curtain Players.

I took my time returning to the dining room, letting my thoughts simmer and mingle together for a minute like Liam's hearty bisque.

I felt like I was getting closer to understanding who might have killed Curtis, and yet I was still unsure I had the right suspect in mind. This was typical at this stage of an investigation and a metaphor for my life. The analytical part of my mind thrived on fitting the nuggets of information I had learned thus far together. At the same time, my emotional center understood that sitting with the uncomfortable not-knowing would ultimately lead to the truth. Lately, I'd been trying to embrace that lesson, accepting that I didn't have to have all of the answers in order to move forward, whether with my deepening relationship with Liam, digging into Scarlet's murder, or deciding what my next career move should be. I thought living in the murky middle, the undefined gray areas, would make me anxious, but the opposite was true. Giving myself permission to let go (even just a little) of my obsessive tendencies was freeing.

THIRTEEN

It took another hour for Dr. Caldwell and her team to finish taking statements and for the power to come back on.

When light flooded the room, everyone cheered.

"You're all free to leave." Dr. Caldwell scanned the table like an eagle stalking its prey from above. "As we've mentioned, we'll be in touch should we need further information from any of you. I would again advise you to stay in Redwood Grove in the short term."

"How long is the short term?" Trishelle asked, bending over to put her heels back on. "I can't stick around here forever. I need to be back at work next week. I wasn't intending to have my visit extended indefinitely. I have a career and responsibilities. This was supposed to be a quick weekend trip."

"Feel free to stop by our offices tomorrow, and we can discuss your travel timeline." Dr. Caldwell shut down any potential response with her answer.

People began filing out of the dining room. Patrick was the first to leave. Jeff started picking up dessert plates with me.

"Put those down," Ophelia scolded, wagging her finger at him.

"Sorry. I guess I'm still in character." He looked at his hands, trying to figure out how the plates had gotten there.

"You're not getting paid to do the dishes." Ophelia wrapped her cape tight around her shoulders. "The curtain has closed on this performance. Go home."

Jeff set the plates back on the table and unbuttoned his chef coat. "I guess I don't need this any longer either. That's it, then? The gig's over. The show is done."

"Can you be any dafter? Of course we're done. We're done for good." Ophelia's cheeks pinched inward. "Give me the costume." She yanked the coat out of his hands and let her cape billow behind her as she exited the room.

Once she was gone, Jeff picked up the dishes again. "I can at least help clear the table."

Why was he sticking around? I couldn't imagine why he would want to linger. He wasn't getting paid as a dishwasher and as Ophelia had said the show was long, long over.

Could it be because he was guilty and trying to eavesdrop on Dr. Caldwell's investigation?

I wondered about the subtext of their exchange. When he asked if the show was done, was he alluding to something bigger? Did he know that the Redwood Curtain Players were about to disband?

Come to think of it, who knew about the theater's financial state aside from Patrick and Ophelia?

Since Jeff wasn't eager to head home, I decided that I might as well use the opportunity to question him.

"That's thoughtful," I said, stacking the dainty, gold-rimmed plates in my arms. "Will you be auditioning for more shows?"

"I don't know. This was my first real break. I was looking forward to putting the acting classes I've taken at the community college into practice tonight. I wonder if I can count this role. Do I have to tell a future director that I didn't actually get to act, or is booking the role enough?" He propped the door open with his foot.

"I'm not familiar with the auditioning process, but telling a director that you had the role isn't a lie. You had the role. Unfortunately, circumstances out of your control canceled the show."

"You wrote a great script, by the way." He waited for me to go into the kitchen first. "It was dense material to work with—real meaty. I've been deep in my character the last couple of weeks preparing for tonight," Jeff said, stepping unevenly around the island. "I've tapped into my inner rage. You should have seen what I was going to do. It was a full circle moment to break free from my timid, awkward chef behavior and then lose it when I got accused of murder. To play a killer, you get to tap into your demons and explore your dark side—it's good to tap into those nasty feelings that lurk in the shadows. I'm bummed I didn't get to show the audience my range, but thank you for writing such a good plot. It's helped me grow as an actor."

"Of course. I'm glad you enjoyed it." I wasn't sure what else to say. My script was bare bones at best and not intended to incite rage. The murder plot was campy and cozy. If Jeff had "tapped into his inner rage," it wasn't because of my script.

Had his timid chef routine been an act? The chewing of his collar? The muttering to the floor?

If that was true, Jeff had been in character all night.

Maybe he was a method actor or a much better character actor than Ophelia gave him credit for.

"You can put those right there." Liam directed Jeff where to set the dishes as we approached the sink.

Curtis's place setting and the other evidence I had gathered were marked and bagged. Yellow evidence markers were scattered throughout the kitchen, and caution tape sealed off the pantry door.

"Well, I guess that's it for me." Jeff plucked at his T-shirt as he skirted past the crime scene evidence. "My short-lived acting career tanked before I had a chance to utter more than a couple of lines, and now I'm jobless, too. What a night. Looks like I'm hitting up all the shops and restaurants tomorrow to see if anyone needs help."

I made space on the counter for my stack. "I thought this was a one-night-only show. How does that make you jobless?"

Jeff flinched ever so slightly at my question, knocking over a wine glass that tumbled over the counter, rolling precariously to the edge. He caught it in one deft movement. "Got it. It's good. It's fine. Nothing broke." He held the glass like a prized trophy to show me.

"No worries." Why had my question rattled him? And why hadn't he answered it? If he had known that the Redwood Curtain Players were losing funding, could he have killed Curtis? His passion for acting was obvious, but the math didn't work. With Curtis dead, his donations would naturally end. Unless there was another financial explanation, like he had a trust set up to support the arts. I made a mental note to ask Dr. Caldwell about Curtis's will. If his remaining estate were set up to be dispersed to the non-profit, that would also give Ophelia a motive for wanting him dead.

"Not broken. Not even a chip," Jeff repeated in a singsong voice like he was getting ready for a musical. "All is good. I should get out of here. I hope you keep writing. You've got an eye for creating unsuspecting villains. I'm bummed I didn't get a chance to showcase just how evil I can be, but maybe another time."

I was struck by how different his behavior was from earlier. What happened to his shifty, skittish, cat-like nerves? His body language and attitude had completely deviated from his baseline at the beginning of the evening.

Was this the real Jeff?

Was everything an act?

He gently laid the glass on its side and scooted away in a rush.

"What was that about?" Liam asked, rinsing plates and stacking them in the dishwasher.

"I'm not sure."

"The kid is skittish." He arranged each item in tidy order, making the linear side of my brain fall harder for him.

"Maybe." I wasn't as convinced. I was starting to wonder if Jeff was a better actor than he let on. Was his jumpiness intentionally masking a hidden rage? Those were his words, not mine. We were assuming his nerves were from the show. That could be exactly what he wanted us to think. What if he was a highly talented actor who was putting on the ultimate performance tonight?

"How can I help?" I asked Liam. The evening was catching up with me. I was ready for my bed. I wanted to get out of my cocktail dress, put on my flannel pajamas, and curl up with Professor Plum and forget about murder for the rest of the night.

"You don't need to help. I've got it." Liam adjusted the top rack of the dishwasher to fit the wine glasses. "Now that we have power, cleanup will be a breeze."

"I'll at least finish clearing the table."

Liam tore his attention away from the sink. "Annie, I can tell you are exhausted. I'm going to run one load and call it a night. Pri and I already talked about it. Everything else can wait until tomorrow. None of us were anticipating that Curtis was going to die. We've been through enough. I'm calling it."

I didn't have the energy to argue.

"Get some rest." His voice changed, softening with his eyes. "Try to sleep."

The tenderness had returned, making it impossible for me to breathe normally. "Yeah, you, too."

Dr. Caldwell repeated the same sentiment when I handed

her my notes. "Thanks for your help, Annie. We have quite a lot to review. I'll be in touch soon, and please don't hesitate to text or call if anything comes up in the meantime."

I said my goodbyes to Pri and Penny, promising that we'd reconvene tomorrow to hash everything out.

Stepping into the cold, dark night was oddly freeing. I stood on the front porch and drank in a long breath, happy to be done with the Wentworth house and relieved to know that the police and Dr. Caldwell were in charge now.

I fought to keep my eyes open on the short drive home. It felt like days had passed. Not hours. The storm had peaked, but driving took every ounce of my concentration. In its retreat, it left huge branches and downed power lines blocking sections of the road. My headlights cut through the darkness, illuminating the slick pavement. Puddles of standing water reflected the tumultuous clouds rolling into the distance. I drove slowly, guided by flashing yellow construction lights and the strong desire to get home and put tonight behind me. Professor Plum and my cozy bed were calling me, and nothing—nothing—was going to deter me now.

FOURTEEN

When I finally turned onto Woodlawn Terrace and my cottage came into view, I nearly burst into tears. I'd been holding it together for hours, and now that I was home, it was like my body knew that it could let go. I steered the car into my driveway. The air was thick with the scent of the rain-soaked earth, and the solar street lamps in our small complex of ten cottages punctuated the cul-de-sac and courtyard with a welcoming touch of warmth.

Professor Plum greeted me at my front door. Never before had I been quite as happy for the sight of the sweet twinkle lights strung along the eaves of my butter-yellow cottage and my favorite furry friend mewing at my feet.

"Good evening, Professor Plum," I said, bending to pick him up. I nuzzled his soft head and kicked off my shoes. "Do you want to hear about tonight? It's a doozy."

I'd had a habit of treating Professor Plum like a human since Scarlet died. He was intended to be her cat. She adopted him shortly before she died, so there was no question that I would take him in. He'd been my faithful companion ever since.

I gave him a handful of his favorite salmon treats and made

myself a cup of rose cardamom tea. Then I curled up on the couch, tucking my feet under a fluffy blanket. Professor Plum made himself at home on my lap, kneading my stomach like bread dough until he was sufficiently comfortable.

"Are you satisfied, sir?" I asked, cradling the tea in my hands.

He meowed in response and adjusted his head so that I could pet it better.

Sometimes, I would almost swear that he was Scarlet reincarnated. His eyes seemed to penetrate through me like he could read my mind.

I sipped my tea and recounted the events of the evening. Like any good listener, Professor Plum stretched his tabby paws and nodded in response every so often. I didn't have a breakthrough or come up with any new theories, but it did feel good to release all the thoughts taking up space in my head.

The problem was I knew myself too well. I wasn't going to be able to let go of Curtis's murder until his killer was behind bars, which was going to distract me from making progress in Scarlet's case.

There's nothing you can do about it tonight, Annie.

I reached for a book, thinking that I might read for a while, but proceeded to fall asleep two pages in.

When I woke the next morning, the storm had blown over, giving way to remarkably blue skies. I padded into the kitchen in my fuzzy slippers and flannel PJs and surveyed the damage out my eating nook windows while I waited for the coffee to brew.

My neighborhood didn't appear to have been hit too hard. Colorful leaves in autumnal tones of cranberry, burnt orange, and maize littered the street and sidewalk like confetti. The professionals would need to remove larger evergreen branches from the redwoods and cedars, but otherwise, the cottages looked like a scene from a warm and cozy fairytale. Chimneys puffed with smoke, and front porches were decorated for Halloween with bales of hay, cornstalks, and pumpkins. Not to be outdone by my fellow residents, I had decked out my cottage with festive purple, orange, and black twinkle lights, a skull wreath, and ghost pumpkins that I planned to carve with Pri and Penny before Halloween.

I could smell cinnamon, nutmeg, and cloves wafting from my neighbor's kitchen. My stomach rumbled in response. Was she baking her famous spiced apple bread? I was one of the youngest residents in our little community, which meant that I was often the lucky recipient of homemade cakes, sweet breads, and pastries.

I loved that age wasn't a barrier for celebrating. Soon trick-or-treaters would fill the village square and spill out into Ocean-side Park for the holiday. Everyone in town joined in the celebration with apple cider tastings, carnival games, face painting, a pub crawl, a costume contest, a pet parade, and a Halloween bake-off.

Last year, I ran out of candy before the stars had even come out. This year, I wasn't making the same mistake. I had already stocked up. Three huge bags of bite-sized chocolate bars and fruity gummies sat atop my fridge. I needed to remember to hide them before Pri came over. She had a serious sweet tooth, especially when she was stressed.

I poured myself a cup of coffee and topped it with a splash of pumpkin spice cream. Professor Plum meowed and rubbed his head against my ankles, signaling that before I savored my coffee, he was in need of his morning kibble and flaked salmon.

A message dinged on my phone as I cozied up on the window bench to drink in the bucolic views while sipping my coffee.

I nearly spilled the rich brew all over me, as I opened the email.

The subject line read: RE: NATALIE THOMPSON'S DISAP-PEARANCE.

Professor Plum, sensing my distress, hopped on my lap, kneaded my stomach, and proceeded to purr as if to tell me he was with me for mutual support.

Natalie Thompson.

I took a large sip of coffee, not caring that it scalded my tongue, and clicked on the email.

Natalie Thompson had gone missing my first year of college. The authorities had never found her body. It's believed that she stumbled upon a corruption scheme involving extremely powerful and high-profile businesspeople that ultimately led to her abduction and presumed murder.

Scarlet and I were assigned her cold case in college. Natalie had been working as an admin for an investment firm in San Francisco at the time of her disappearance. She had reached out to the local police department about concerns that her employer was involved in illegal activities. The police filed a report, but never followed up.

I'd read the report in question at least forty times, and every time I reviewed it, I was filled with anger. The officer's personal biases and dismissal of Natalie were evident in the way he referred to her as "a pretty young woman without a college degree or much business sense."

How dare he?

He blew off Natalie's claims, noting that she'd watched too many crime shows and had an overactive imagination. He also implied that she'd had an affair with her boss and was a woman on a mission to seek revenge.

None of that matched what Scarlet and I learned while reviewing the case notes. A new team of detectives compiled interviews with Natalie's friends, family, and co-workers after she vanished without a trace and painted a different picture. One of a vibrant woman who was eager to learn. She'd been social and outgoing. Employee reviews from her first two years working at the firm were glowing. She'd received raises, promotions, and bonuses.

Something changed the year she went missing. Her friends and family reported that she became withdrawn. She lost weight, wasn't sleeping, wasn't eating. One of the worst interviews was with Natalie's mom, who was so concerned about her daughter's well-being that she'd reached out to various medical professionals and therapists.

It was heartbreaking to read and made all the worse by the fact that had the police taken her seriously from the beginning, she might still be alive today.

As the analytical member of our two-person detective squad, I initially broke all of the information we received about the case from Dr. Caldwell into bitesize, trackable pieces. Scarlet became consumed by the case but on an almost personal level. Our roles became even more cemented our last semester. She took it upon herself to reach out to Natalie's parents, friends, co-workers, and some of the officers assigned to her case.

"Someone is going to slip, Annie. I can feel it. People are scared. I need to get them to trust me. Then they'll talk."

Whatever she was working on before she was killed, she kept it close to her chest. "It's a surprise. I've got big news, but I need to firm up a few things before I can tell you."

Except she never had a chance to firm anything up or tell me what she had discovered.

Getting new information made the case feel alive again. Natalie's vanishment was the catalyst and the key to everything. If I could trace what happened to her, I just might be able to track down Scarlet's killer. They had to be one and the same.

It was as if Natalie's death had repeated with Scarlet.

Scarlet made the same mistakes. Whatever she had discovered put her in harm's way. If only she would have confided in me. Maybe we could have solved it together—or I could have somehow at least kept her safe.

After she died, I couldn't let it go. I spent days, weeks, years retracing her last movements, reviewing her homework assignments, and trying to figure out what in the world she could have uncovered that scared—no, terrified—Natalie's assailant into killing again.

Every direction led to a dead end. That was until a few months ago when Liam watched Professor Plum for the night while I was stuck in a hospital bed with a mild concussion. Professor Plum's collar had come loose. Liam had been unduly worried I'd be upset with him, but the truth was that I hadn't changed his collar since Scarlet first brought the tiny tabby kitten to our apartment. The memory was etched into my brain. I took another long sip of my pumpkin spice coffee, recalling the late spring afternoon when Scarlet had shown up at our apartment with a tabby kitten the size of my palms.

"Is he the cutest thing you've ever seen, Annie?" Scarlet beamed as she cradled him like a baby. "We have to come up with a clever name. Something mysterious. Something that will blend with our detective agency. He's going to be our mascot. Every good detective needs a sidekick."

"I thought I was your sidekick?"

"No, we're going to be equal partners in our new endeavor. This little guy will greet our clients and purr in their laps while we extract secrets from them." She winked and kissed the top of his head.

"What about Professor Plum?" I suggested. "Professor Plum and Scarlet."

"I love it," she squealed. "But what about you? Don't you want your name reflected in our business name, too?"

"Have you met me?" I scrunched my forehead. "I would

much prefer *not* to have my name in lights or basically anywhere."

"It's fate. Look at this. It's perfect. It's plum." She chuckled and reached into her pocket to remove a deep purple expandable cat collar. "And, Annie, you'll eventually have to get over that. We're going to run a high-powered, kick-ass, all-female detective agency. You can't hide in the background behind me forever. You're a mastermind. People need to know that."

"I'm quite content letting you be the face of our agency," I insisted. "It's the dream setup for me."

I stood to refill my coffee and glanced out the window, struck by the way the trees and grass in the shared courtyard sparkled with the morning dew. There was no questioning Redwood Grove's simple beauty. It was one of the many reasons I had come to call this place home, and I wanted to do everything in my power to make sure our village and the people I had come to care for so dearly were safe.

Curtis's murder loomed heavy.

I wondered what it might have been like if Scarlet and I had opened our detective agency. Surely, she would have pushed to take on the case. Not that she would have needed to push hard. I was always game to investigate with her.

I chuckled at the thought of her needing to twist my arm as I stirred more pumpkin spice cream into my coffee and returned to the window seat.

Scarlet and I balanced each other. It was the thing that made us such great friends and business partners. Scarlet was effortlessly vivacious and easygoing, with the kind of magnetic personality that drew you in. I was more methodical, internal, and bookish. But one thing I had come to understand was how much I had grown and changed in the last decade. I wasn't the same young woman who questioned her worth and ability. I didn't need Scarlet to pull me out of my shell. I had cracked myself open since moving to Redwood Grove.

"We've done that together, huh, Professor Plum," I said, petting his back as he jumped up to take command of the window scene.

He matched his collar and his name. And he may have been intended for Scarlet, but he became my cat the day she died. She was our point of connection. We had grown up together without her.

I glanced at his new collar. It was black and white with skulls and crossbones, fitting for a tabby named after the Clue character.

I still couldn't believe that the sparkly purple collar he'd worn around his neck for almost a decade had a hidden compartment that Scarlet had used to stash her intel on Natalie Thompson. When Liam brought me the collar in the hospital, I wasn't upset that it had broken. I was devastated it had taken me so long to realize the last clue Scarlet left for me had been hiding in plain sight, right in front of me.

The worst part was that she must have known that she was walking into danger. Why would she have hidden the chip in Professor Plum's collar otherwise?

Her notes and interviews with Natalie's co-workers were on it. One of them, a man who asked to remain anonymous, whom she referred to as Bob, scheduled a meeting with her the afternoon she killed.

I'd been searching for Bob's true identity ever since, but Scarlet had been trained by the best—Dr. Caldwell. Nowhere in her notes was there so much as a mention to anyone other than Bob. She had been meticulously careful to protect her killer.

That really stung, but it hadn't stopped me. I sent inquiries to other co-workers. The problem was that so much time had passed that people had moved on.

Professor Plum's meows demanding attention brought me back into the moment and made me realize I couldn't hold off the inevitable.

I took another long, slow sip of coffee, mustering the courage to read the email.

Please don't let this be another dead end.

FIFTEEN

My fingers trembled as I scrolled through the email.

Annie, thank you for your note. I'm sorry it's taken me a while to respond. I don't check this account very often. I left Silicon Summit Partners the year after Natalie disappeared and moved to the East Coast. I'm not sure how much I can offer in terms of insight, but I'll be in the Bay Area next month and would be happy to meet for a coffee. My cell is below. Feel free to text me, and we can coordinate a date and time to connect.

All the best,

Mark Vincent

I reread the message three times.
This is it!
Finally.
A break.
I'd found Mark's name on an old list of Silicon Summit Partners employees. I knew it was a long shot, but I had emailed

everyone on the list in hopes that someone might have a clue as to Bob's real identity.

Most people had been polite in declining my request for information. This was the first person who actually agreed to speak with me, and in person, no less.

Although, was there something to that?

Could Mark want to meet me while he was traveling because he had information he didn't feel safe sharing via email?

"We can't be too careful about this meeting," I said to Professor Plum, locking my phone screen and drinking every remaining drop of coffee.

I had a month to strategize. I intended to learn everything I could about Mark Vincent's background and figure out the safest place to meet him. It would need to be somewhere very public and during the daytime, but also a spot that would provide at least some sense of privacy so that if he did have information about Natalie or Scarlet to share, he would feel safe to do so.

Professor Plum jumped off my lap as a knock sounded on the door.

My hunch was correct. My neighbor stood waiting with a loaf of apple spice bread in her hands. She was in her early eighties with silver hair, deep dimples, and the kind of smile that made you want to lean into her arms for a hug.

"Good morning, dear. I hope I'm not waking you, but you know me, I'm up before the sun most mornings, and last night's deluge called for my famous apple spice bread. Can I tempt you with some? I baked way too much." She held the tin in her wrinkled hands like a special offering. Her sweater looked as if it had been knitted by hand. Its maroons and browns blended in with the foliage around us.

My mouth watered with anticipation. "I could smell it

while I was enjoying my coffee, and I was hoping that you might have a slice to spare."

She beamed with delight and thrust the tin at me. "Slice, Annie? You get your own loaf. There's more where that came from, so don't be shy."

"Thank you." I happily took the bread, resisting the temptation to tear off a hunk immediately. "I'm just afraid that I might eat the entire pan before I go to the bookstore." It was a good sign she didn't mention anything about last night's events. Hopefully, that meant word hadn't spread widely through town yet. News and gossip tended to travel quickly in Redwood Grove, but a little reprieve this morning would be nice.

She gave me a conspiratorial wink and pressed a wrinkled finger to her lips. "Do it. I'll never tell. Your secret is safe with me."

I laughed and gave her a hug, promising to check to see if any new copies of Stephen King's latest thriller had come in. I loved that my eighty-year-old neighbor spoiled me with homemade bread and that she had a penchant for dark and gory fiction.

After helping myself to two large slices of the sweet bread packed with tangy chunks of tart apples, I changed into a pair of leggings, T-shirt and an oversized knee-length cardigan, and my boots for the walk to the bookstore.

The distraction of receiving a response from Mark had taken my mind off Curtis's murder. I took the long route to the store through Oceanside Park. Walking through the park was my morning meditation, a time to silence my inner narrator and take in the stunning display of nature. My feet sank into the squishy bark dust as I navigated the tree-lined pathway, stepping over fragrant boughs of evergreens. The park looked like it belonged on a travel postcard with its vibrant red Japanese maples and crisp changing yellow leaves clinging to the black oaks.

The park was the centerpiece for community gatherings, with miles of trails that stretched up into the surrounding redwoods, a pavilion for outdoor movies and concerts in the summer, water features, play structures, and native California plants and flowers that attracted hummingbirds and butterflies. We might be a thirty-minute drive to the coast, but the air was infused with the smell of saltwater and damp earth. Tree branches and small bushes uprooted in the storm littered the lush, dewy grass. Rare puddles of water pooled in the children's play area. The entire state of California had been in a permanent drought for the last decade, so I refused to complain about any rain.

My thoughts drifted to Liam. Had we really nearly kissed, or was my imagination playing tricks on me? A few months ago I would have said that Liam Donovan was the last person on the planet I would want to kiss. Now I couldn't stop thinking about his soft, full lips brushing against mine or running my fingers through his wavy hair.

If Dr. Caldwell hadn't shown up, what might have happened?

I let out a wistful sigh.

Let it go, Annie.

Fall tucked our little village square in like a warm hug. Red-tiled rooftops glistened along Cedar Avenue. A mix of midcentury modern, California coastal, and Spanish architecture gave downtown an eclectic charm. Terra cotta pots overflowing with cheerful fall floral displays lined the sidewalks. Banners announcing the Halloween festivities hung from lampposts.

Storefronts were decked out for the holiday with paper skeletons, bats, and pumpkins hanging in the windows. Shop owners were already up and sweeping their sidewalks. City trucks rumbled down the street, clearing debris. A line had formed in front of State of Mind Public House for their Saturday morning brunch. Part of me wanted to jump in line and join them because the smell of bacon and sourdough pancakes was intoxicating.

Anytime I walked through the village, I was reminded of how lucky I was to live in a place like this. It made me even more resolved to figure out who had killed Curtis. I loved that our small town had a natural sense of calm. Last night's murder had thrown that off balance, and I was uniquely qualified to help bring Curtis's killer to justice.

I turned off Cedar Avenue onto the long gravel drive that led to the Secret Bookcase. The bookshop was in an English manor house that Hal Christie, my boss, had converted many years ago. This section of the walk always made me feel like I was in the pages of a Jane Austen novel. A formal gate was propped open, inviting readers to venture down the path lined with ancient ivy and wisteria. A formal English garden sat to my right. Hal insisted that the gardens remained open to the public when he took over the property.

At this time of year, there wasn't much blooming, but that didn't take away from the majestic topiaries, carved stone benches, rose bushes, wild grasses, red spider lilies, and bubbling fountains. The grounds stretched as far as I could see. Another stipulation from Hal was that the trails connecting to the park's west side also stayed accessible to the community. He encouraged locals and visitors to meander the pathways or linger in the garden with a crisp iced tea and shortbread cookie. Preserving open spaces was one of his passions, which aligned beautifully with his deep interest in all things Agatha Christie.

"Readers should be able to wander and get lost in the pages of a book amongst our blooming jasmines," he would say. "These hallowed grounds could produce the next Agatha. While I'm at the helm, the Secret Bookcase will always belong to the people. Who knows, an aspiring writer could be penning the next great American mystery out in the garden right now."

Hal's enthusiasm for accessibility was contagious. As was

his insistence that he was the long-lost grandson of Ms. Christie herself. His theory stemmed from the fact that Agatha Christie had gone missing for eleven days in her mid-thirties. No one had ever officially solved the mystery of her short-lived disappearance. Some believed it was an elaborate publicity stunt, while others suggested that she was attempting to exact her revenge on her husband, who was about to divorce her. Hal was convinced that she had given birth to a baby during her vanishing act and that *said baby* was his mother. The math worked, and some of the extraneous details he'd learned about his mother's adoption lined up with Agatha's disappearance. Still, no other expert had raised the idea that the world's most famous mystery writer had a secret love child.

Next summer, Hal was taking us across the pond to the Old Swan Hotel in Harrogate for the world's largest celebration of crime writing. It would be good research for the bookstore, especially as we leaned into offering more events and interactive author talks and workshops. I knew that Hal was eager to visit the site where Agatha was found. He was hoping to find answers to his past. Something I knew all too well. I just hoped he wouldn't be too devastated if the truth didn't align with his vision.

I pushed the thought aside as I reached the entrance to the bookstore. The manor house never failed to take my breath away. The two-story building, adorned with ivy and climbing roses, had a touch of romance all year round. Large bay windows graced the entrance, which was marked by an arched wooden door and a brass plaque with skull and crossbones that read: THE SECRET BOOKCASE—ENTER AT YOUR OWN RISK.

Halloween bunting and Edison-style light bulbs were strung from the house across the gravel walk. A gothic wreath twisted with grapevines, black feathers, and dried oranges hung on the door. Inflatable spiders the size of small cars crawled up the front walls and peered over the roofline with their creepy, buggy eyes. Hal had decorated with the massive inflatables long before I started working at the bookstore. Halloween was his favorite holiday, and he had always gone out of his way to transform the shop into an inviting yet spooky haunted mansion.

Silhouettes of ghosts clung to the second-story windows, and two witch's cauldrons overflowing with wrapped candies flanked either side of the front door.

I let myself in and turned on the lights in the Foyer. A soft smile spread across my face. Every time I stepped inside the bookshop, it felt like coming home. There was no place on the planet, at least in my humble opinion, quite as peaceful, snug, and cozy.

Immediately upon entering the Secret Bookcase, readers were greeted with tea and coffee service and a collection of bookish merchandise like poison mugs, library-scented candles, and quill pens. The cash register divided the space from the Conservatory, the ballroom where we hosted our large author talks and signings.

For Halloween, the coffee table had been draped with velvet black tablecloths and gauzy spiderwebs. A witch's broom scented with cinnamon hung next to the bay windows, with dozens of tiny fake plastic spiders scurrying up to the ceiling. That had been Fletcher's idea and the effect had turned out better than I expected.

I started a pot of coffee and warmed water for tea. Then I set out an assortment of cookies and biscotti and lit the electric candles on the bookshelves. By the time I had reviewed our inventory sheet for the day, Hal padded into the Foyer, cradling a mug of chai in his hands.

"Well, you're up and at 'em early this morning, Annie." His blue eyes crinkled when he smiled. Hal was in his late sixties with a neatly trimmed white beard, gray hair, and a penchant for cardigans. He had an encyclopedic knowledge of mysteries and the authors who had penned them and could recommend the perfect book for any reader who happened into the store.

It was clear from his cheery and upbeat greeting he couldn't have heard the news about Curtis. I hated having to be the one to tell him. Knowing Hal and his deep love for Redwood Grove, I had a feeling he was going to take Curtis's murder hard. I would need to fill him in gently. "Have you heard about what happened last night?" I asked, pouring myself a cup of coffee.

"No, and I don't like the tone in your voice, my dear." The lines on Hal's forehead were etched with concern as he stared at me, waiting for more.

I told him about Curtis's murder while I poured a splash of cream and a packet of honey into my coffee. I probably didn't need the extra caffeine, but after last night, a little extra buzz of energy wouldn't hurt.

"That's terrible." Hal rested his tea on the counter and came closer to pat my shoulder in a show of support. "I'm sorry you had to witness that. How are you doing? Should you be here?"

He was like a grandfather to me. I leaned into his shoulder. "Thanks, Hal. It was shocking, to say the least, but I think work will be good for me. I need the distraction, and I promised Dr. Caldwell that I'd help her with the investigation."

"Of course you did." Hal gave me a squeeze and released me. "Are there any clear leads or suspects?"

"Unfortunately, not yet. I have a few people on my list, but until we know what killed him and when he ingested the poison, it's a bit of a guessing game."

"Guessing games are where you shine, Annie." Hal lifted his teacup in praise.

"I just wish it was less guessing and more facts at this stage," I said.

The doorbell jingled. We turned to see my friend and colleague Fletcher coming into the store, dressed for the elements in a long, black, hooded rain jacket, and a golf umbrella tucked under his arm. "Did I hear mention of facts? Are you in need of a fact-checker? Because you know that's my specialty."

Hal busied himself unpacking a new delivery of books, giving me space to share (or not) the gory details from last night. Fletcher was as much family to me as Hal. We were each other's found family. The Secret Bookcase brought us together, and years of working side by side gave us the opportunity to strengthen our connection. Never underestimate the power of time and proximity.

I knew all of Fletcher's quirks, and he knew mine. We were more like brother and sister than coworkers. Fletcher was messy, disorganized, a walking Sherlockian dictionary, and a collector of miniatures. This month, his side of our shared office had been taken over by a four-foot-tall LEGO haunted mansion. In his spare time, he tinkered with the project, adding extra bricks and embellishments like chaining plastic mummies to the upper turrets.

I'm organized to a fault. Clutter gives me heart palpitations. I'm sure a therapist could help me unpack why my anxiety spikes with chaos. It's probably due to my analytical mindset and need to control my environment. My parents owned a diner when I was growing up. They loved me and still do, I never doubted that—but they were busy running a commercial kitchen and keeping their small business afloat. I learned to rely on myself at a young age. Teachers at school recognized my innate talent for solving puzzles and tasked me with harder problems that I would spend hours trying to work through after school, tucked into a red vinyl booth munching on curly fries and a milkshake.

In hindsight, I realize that having uninterrupted time for my brain to wander, ruminate, and mull over challenges helped me hone the skills I have today. I didn't know it at the time, but boredom was a gift. Countless hours of lingering in my head, running through imaginary problems, taught me how to deliberate. Those long afternoons when my legs would stick to the vinyl cushions were my residency in people-watching. While I would doodle in my spiral-bound notebook, I paid careful attention to conversations in the restaurant, keeping copious notes on body language, practicing lip reading, and trying to figure out tells.

Although Fletcher might say my need to keep things compartmentalized and in neat and tidy boxes was over-the-top.

He set his umbrella next to the coat rack. "What's with the long face?"

I pressed my lips together and raised my eyebrows, shaking my head. It was still hard to come to terms with the fact that Curtis had dropped dead in the middle of our dinner party. "You won't believe it. There was a murder last night."

"A murder? Where?" Fletcher's intelligent eyes darted from the front display to the Conservatory as if he were looking for the outline of a dead body.

"Not here," I assured him before giving him the recap of dinner.

"That's too on the nose for Liam." Fletcher tapped the side of his long, narrow nose. "It screams of *The Hound of the Baskervilles*, a remote house, a howling storm. Was he out searching for wild beasts?"

"What?" I stared at him with confusion. "What does *The Hound of the Baskervilles* have to do with Liam? He doesn't read mysteries."

Fletcher threw his hand over his mouth and stumbled over his words. "Did I say Liam? Did you say Liam? No. Nothing. Never mind. I don't know what I'm saying. Where's the coffee? I need coffee."

A vision of Liam stuffing something that strongly resembled

a gilded book into the tub last night popped into my mind. "Fletcher, is Liam reading Sherlock?"

"Huh?" Fletcher cupped his hand over his ear. "Is that the phone?"

"No way! Liam *is* reading *The Hound of the Baskervilles.*" Fletcher had no poker face.

"He swore me to secrecy." Fletcher zipped his lips. "You're not supposed to know. Please don't tell him I let it slip."

"Your secret is safe with me." I couldn't hide the small grin spreading across my face. Nor could I believe Liam was stooping so low as to read a mystery. How sweet.

Maybe I would have to put in a special order for some historical non-fiction. If Liam was reading my favorite genre, it was only fair for me to read his.

"That's uncanny timing about Curtis," Fletcher said changing the subject. He took off his coat and hung it on the rack. "I saw him yesterday."

"You saw Curtis, where?"

"At Cryptic. Hal and I decided we needed chai lattes to weather the storm, so I offered to brave the elements and walk over for a late-afternoon cinnamon spice. You were already setting up for the dinner, and that high school kid was taking over for Pri. Let's just say that our chais did not compare to hers. They were fine, but it did make me appreciate how much talent is involved in being a barista."

I knew Pri would be pleased to hear that.

"In any event, Curtis was railing on a poor guy who was there dropping off his résumé. The guy was a chef. I thought that Cryptic already had an in-house baker, but—" Fletcher brushed imaginary drops of rain from his long-sleeved eighties-style raven-and-heather-gray T-shirt with a single question mark in the center. "I think he must have known the guy. It sounded like maybe he had worked for Curtis. I'm not sure. I didn't stick around long enough to find out, but Curtis was making a scene.

I felt bad for the barista because he had no control over the situation. Pri would have shut that down."

"What did the guy look like?" I asked, already forming an idea of who Curtis might have been arguing with in my head.

"Mid-twenties, sort of jumpy."

I had a feeling I knew exactly who he was talking about. "Was he wearing a white chef's coat?"

Fletcher snapped his finger and thumb together. "Yes, that's it. You've hit the nail on the coffin, clever Annie. How did you deduce this with such little information to go on?"

I rolled my eyes and shook my head. Once Fletcher shifted into Sherlock mode, there was no stopping him. "That's Jeff. He's not a chef. He's an actor who was hired to play the chef last night."

"Aha, the plot thickens." Fletcher rubbed his hands together eagerly.

Hal gave him a short shake of the head to tell him to stop.

I appreciated that he was trying to protect me, but honestly Fletcher's lightness was exactly what I needed. "So Curtis and Jeff were arguing at the coffee shop before dinner."

"I wouldn't say arguing," Fletcher interrupted. "Curtis was doing all of the talking while Jeff stood there quivering and taking the battery of insults without comment."

Questions swarmed my mind. What were Curtis and Jeff arguing about? Why was Jeff already distributing his résumé? Could it be tied to the murder? Last night Jeff sounded like his unemployment was new. If that were true, then why was he already job hunting?

SIXTEEN

I didn't have time to dwell on Jeff's employment status or the fact that Liam was secretly reading Sherlock because we were due to open the store. Hal left to turn on lights in each of the themed book rooms. Fletcher updated the sandwich board we propped in front of the store with a Halloween quote from Count Dracula: LISTEN TO THEM—THE CHILDREN OF THE NIGHT. WHAT MUSIC THEY MAKE!

"We're going to need to have the gothic playlist on rotation today," he said, adding music notes with a flourish to the chalkboard. Fletcher's talent for calligraphy never failed to impress me. "Did you remember that we have the special Halloween story time for the kids this morning with a few of the actors from the Redwood Curtain Players? That starts at eleven. I was going to set up everything in the Dig Room before closing last night, but Hal thinks we'll get a large turnout and wants to do it in the Conservatory."

"I forgot about that, but I can set it up." I wondered who was coming from the Redwood Curtain Players. It might be an opportunity for me to have another conversation with Ophelia or Jeff.

"Okay, I'll put the sign outside and take the helm at the cash register." Fletcher brushed chalk from his fingers and went outside.

I hoped Jeff or Ophelia showed up. The mystique of the Wentworth estate was hard to shake. Locals swore the Wentworth family was cursed. Could their bad luck be attached to the house? After sitting empty for decades, the first time Penny reopened the doors, a murder had occurred. It was most likely a coincidence, but I wasn't a fan of coincidences. And I most certainly wasn't a fan of my friends and people I cared about being in danger.

Sunlight flooded through the tall, arched windows in the ballroom. The mint green walls and polished wood floors shimmered with sparkling natural light like the great room had been bedazzled with tiny gemstones. Bookshelves with our newest releases took up the far corner of the space. I pushed the couches and cozy chairs into the center of the room in front of the stage. Then, I rolled out the cart of folding chairs we kept in the storage closet and arranged them in rows. I moved the Halloween display of pumpkins and scarecrows to the side of the stage to make room for the actors. Since this was a children's event, I set up a folding table in front of the windows for snacks. I covered the table with a black tablecloth and arranged plates of cookies and crackers and jugs of apple cider.

"This looks lovely," Hal said, strolling into the room with an armful of middle-grade mysteries. "Do you think you could figure out a spot for these?"

"Of course." I took them out of his hands. "Should I grab any other kids' titles from the Dig Room?"

"There is a special order of board books and early readers for the youngsters that came in, but it's up in the overstock room. If you wouldn't mind grabbing it, these old, creaky knees would thank you. They don't seem to love the rain. It's a good thing we live in California." He patted his corduroy pants.

"No problem. I'm on it."

"You're on top of everything, Annie, which worries me." Hal's smile faded. He pushed up the sleeves of his cardigan and stared wistfully out toward the garden.

"Why?"

His voice wobbled with emotion. "You know I can't run the store forever. I'll be seventy soon. Where do the years go? In my mind, I'm as spry as I was in my forties, but then we get a cold, wet, windy night like last night and my joints decide that they're going to seize up on me."

"Can you take something? Are you in a lot of pain?" His back was to me, so I couldn't tell if he was masking how much he was actually hurting.

"No, no. It's nothing that serious. The sun is already helping. I'm like an old, rusty bike that needs a good oiling." He let out a slight laugh, but kept his gaze focused on the grounds. "At some point in the near future, we should sit down and talk about your plans."

"My plans?" I didn't like the sound of this. What was he hinting at?

He rolled his shoulders and turned to face me. "You and Fletcher are the body and soul of the store. If neither of you want to continue to keep it open after I retire, well..." He trailed off. "Then I suppose we'll have to cross that bridge when we come to it."

Liam Donovan, among others, had shown interest in purchasing the manor house a while back. I knew that Hal could probably sell the property and retire with ease. I hated the thought that he was hanging on to it for me, but I also couldn't fathom the idea of Redwood Grove without the Secret Bookcase.

"I don't want to put any extra pressure on you, Annie. I'm not in a hurry to make any decisions right away." He slapped his thighs like he was trying to encourage blood to flow. "Yesterday was a reminder that I'm not getting any younger, that's all."

I knew that wasn't "all" of what we needed to discuss. I was worried that Hal might be struggling more than he was letting on. He wasn't getting any younger and I could tell the long days in the store were taking a toll. He deserved to enjoy and savor his golden years. I didn't want him to keep the store for our sake.

I couldn't drag out a decision about my future much longer. It wasn't fair to Hal, Dr. Caldwell, or myself. I just wished there was a way I could do both. Was it feasible to run my own private detective agency and keep working at the Secret Bookcase? Fletcher wasn't going anywhere. He would stay at the bookstore forever if was a possibility. Maybe we could hire a couple of extra part-time staff—high school or college students. It could work. I needed to give it some thought.

"Enough of my rambling. Ignore this old man." Hal waved me toward the stairs. "We're about to be bombarded by troops of costumed, candy-hungry readers. We better batten down the hatches and prepare."

"True. Prepare for the invasion of ghosts, goblins, and spooks galore. Scary witches knocking at our door. Wait, am I unintentionally rhyming?" I grinned and made a goofy face, happy for a moment of normalcy.

"That's what kids' programming will do to you." Hal winked.

I paused before going upstairs and placed my hand over my chest. "Thanks for being honest with me. I know we have a lot to discuss, and I'm ready whenever you are."

Hal shoved his hands in his pockets. "Let's get through the holiday, and then we'll talk."

I smiled and left him, feeling eternally grateful that he was willing to have a conversation about keeping the Secret Bookcase open. Whether I was ready or not, the universe was nudging me forward—or maybe about to push me off a cliff. Either way, it was time for me to start doing some soul-searching in the form of spreadsheets. I needed to map out exactly how much time and staffing would be required if Fletcher and I were in charge of the bookstore and compare that with the costs and work that would need to go into opening my own agency. Plus, I still needed to sit with the idea of working directly for Dr. Cald-well. I felt like it was the lowest on my list, but I needed to compare and contrast the pros and cons of each decision to feel confident in determining which route was best for me.

For the moment, I needed to prepare to entertain our tiniest readers. The actors were due to arrive anytime, and soon we'd have a crowd of families eagerly awaiting a special immersive Halloween story hour.

I hurried upstairs and retrieved the boxes of children's mysteries. Then I finished arranging a cute display next to the snack table with books, stickers, bookmarks, mystery board games, puzzles, and stuffed plush Scooby-Doo characters.

My heart swelled when kids in costumes began streaming in. Happy chatter filled the cavernous ballroom. One younger reader was dressed as Nate the Great, complete with a trench coat, checkered hat, magnifying glass, and toy dog. Fairies flitted around the dance floor, and young witches in pointy hats cast spells with plastic wands.

"I don't particularly like kids, but I have to admit this is fairly adorable," Fletcher said under his breath, bringing in a fresh tray of cutout cookies. His cerebral approach to reading was better matched with an adult audience who could dissect the nuances of sentence structure and discuss literary pros, but I was glad even he had a soft spot for our burgeoning readers. They were the future of the store, and just knowing that a new generation was getting swept up into the love of a book gave me hope.

"The actors are ready and waiting in the Parlor if you want to make the welcome announcement." Fletcher wasn't asking. Speaking in front of an audience, especially a twelve-and-under audience, wasn't his forte.

"No problem." I walked up to the stage and tapped on the mic to get everyone's attention. "Welcome to the Secret Book-case, readers. We have a special story time for you today, but before we bring out our surprise guests, let's take a minute to show off your amazing costumes. If you're wearing a costume, please stand." I led the applause. Kids beamed with pride as they waved during their moment of recognition.

"Wonderful. And remember, be sure to stop at the book table in the back and get a free sticker." More applause sounded. "Now, you're going to be detectives. I'm going to give you a clue about who's reading your story today. Let's see if you can guess who it is." I reached under the podium and lifted up a Dalmatian stuffed animal.

"Dogs!" one kid shouted.

"Dalmatian," another added.

"Close. Any other detectives with a guess?" I waited.

One girl seated in the very back row who was dressed like a porcupine raised her hand. "Cruella de Vil?"

"That's right. You are a super sleuth." I used both my hands to motion toward the Foyer. "Let's welcome the one and only Cruella de Vil."

Kids screamed, covered their eyes, and jumped up and down as Ophelia marched into the room wearing a black-and-white wig, red gloves, and a fur cape. She held a long, fake cigarette holder in one hand and pounced on the kids in the front row. This made the audience erupt in joyful screams again.

I watched in awe as she commanded the audience. Jeff played the role of her henchman, Jasper. His ratty brown coat and hat made him look the part of a crook. His performance was equally compelling and completely different than his role last night.

Gone was any sign of his skittish nerves or chewing on his coat.

Again I found myself wondering, was Jeff a much better actor than he let on?

Was he confirming my theory right in front of my eyes?

Ophelia was almost too convincing as a Disney villain. She embodied the part with ease, taking great pleasure in making the poor, unsuspecting readers in the first two rows duck and hide every time she pretended to snatch the stuffed Dalmatian out of Jeff's hands.

As far as story times went, this was one of the most engaging and interactive kids' events we'd hosted in a long time. I was glad for Hal. I knew seeing the kids in costume brought the Halloween magic to life for him. But I couldn't shake the feeling that fiction was paralleling reality.

Was I seeing the real Ophelia?

Did Jeff have a darker side that he could clearly tap into when the role required it?

Another thought took hold as they finished the reading, and I scooted to the snack and book tables to hand out stickers and help families find new Halloween reads to bring home. What if the two of them had teamed up to murder Curtis? Watching them transform into different people was a red flag when it came to killing. Ophelia had dismissed her actors' abilities. She had made it clear that community theater attracted amateurs. Was that an intentional distraction? Did she want me to think that so that I didn't pay attention to the fact that both of them were much more talented than they first let on?

I kept my eyes on the stage while I finished passing out stickers and encouraging kids to take an extra cookie. I wanted a chance to speak with them alone before they took off again. I needed to learn more about the Redwood Curtain Players. Was it all an act? Could the spider in the drink right before Curtis died have been a sleight of hand performed by a trained actor to keep all eyes off of the real crime? I wasn't sure yet, but I knew that Ophelia and Jeff were solidly on my list of potential suspects, and I intended to get as much out of them as I could.

SEVENTEEN

Once kids and families trickled out of the store, I found Jeff and Ophelia huddled in the Sitting Room on my way to restock children's titles. Stepping into the sweet and charming reading room was like stepping into the pages of a Miss Marple novel. Floral wallpaper designed to resemble the elderly sleuth's house in St. Mary Mead gave the space a welcoming, grandmotherly feel. Wingback chairs and bench seating with cushy pillows offered readers a space to curl up for the afternoon with a bundle of knitting and a cup of tea. Runners and throw rugs stretched between the bookshelves, and pastoral black-and-white photographs of the English countryside circa the 1940s lined the walls.

The Sitting Room was arguably the most popular spot in the Secret Bookcase since it housed our piece-de-resistance—an actual secret bookshelf. Neither Ophelia nor Jeff was interested in the hidden compartment, though. They were deep in conversation with their backs to the door. They had pushed two chairs together so close that their heads were nearly touching.

"Am I interrupting?" I asked as a way of announcing my presence.

Ophelia flinched, yanking her body away from Jeff. She recovered effortlessly, like any good actor. "Not at all, dear. This is your store. We were simply reviewing notes from this morning's performance, weren't we, Jeff?"

Jeff mumbled a response and scooted his chair away from hers.

This was my chance to see if I could extract any new information from them. The sooner I could help solve Curtis's murder the sooner our sweet village could return to normalcy. Story time was a perfect example of what life in Redwood Grove was usually like. I wanted more costumed kids munching on Halloween cookies and fewer poisoned vials and guests dropping dead at dinner.

I watched them carefully, as I smiled brightly. "The kids loved it. You were both very convincing. Hal already said it needs to become an annual Halloween event." I readjusted the stack of books in my arms that needed to be shelved in the Dig Room. "We sold almost all of our inventory."

"Wonderful." Ophelia puffed on the tip of her fake cigarette like she was still in character. "Sadly, I'm afraid it will be impossible to commit to a date that far out. The fate of the Redwood Curtain Players is up in the air. Last night might have been our final curtain call. Our funding has run dry, and unless we can tap into a new well, I'm not sure we'll be operating this time next year."

I couldn't believe she was being so forthcoming about their financial issues, but I certainly wasn't going to tell her I'd already heard this news from Patrick. "That's terrible. Doesn't most of your funding come from the community and ticket sales from performances?"

The purple veins in her neck bulged as she muttered something unintelligible under her breath before responding. "Ticket sales barely cover the cost of costuming, set production, and renting the venue. We have a partnership with the Wentworth Trust. The museum gives us the performance hall at a steep discount. Ticket sales typically cover that, but not much else. We rely heavily on community donations for the rest, hence why it's called community theater."

"What about paying the actors?" I looked at Jeff.

He deferred to Ophelia with a shrug. "We don't get paid. Last night was a bonus. Thank you again for the stipend."

"The thanks belong to Penny, not me. She wanted to make sure that everyone was compensated."

"We appreciate that kind of generosity." Ophelia gave Jeff a pointed look to signal him to stop talking. "It's always a delight to be able to offer our community actors payment for their time. That's my pitch to our donors. People don't understand the vast amount of work that happens behind the scenes to put on a performance. Our volunteer actors spend hours and hours learning lines, rehearsing, and helping build sets, you name it. It's often a thankless job, but the payoff is the audience's reaction. It's tremendously rewarding to be greeted with applause and a standing ovation at the end of a performance. I think one could argue that community theater is the *truest* form of theater. Our actors are in it for the art, not the money."

Her impassioned speech sounded rehearsed. I wondered if this was the pitch she used when trying to drum up more money.

"Up until the last few months, we've been fortunate to have community partners who understood the mission and the importance of maintaining thriving arts programming." She was nearly breathless when she finished, her cheeks flushed with red, and her movements jerky.

"But that changed?" I prompted.

She tossed her fake cigarette holder on the walnut coffee table and took off her wig. Her hair was plastered to her head with a nylon cap. She shook it free. "Word is going to spread. There's no keeping anything a secret, so you might as well hear it from me. Yes, that changed because Curtis pulled his funding at the beginning of the month, basically leaving us out in the cold."

Jeff sat stoically. Not a muscle moved in his body. Not a twitch of the eye or a shift of the shoulders. His posture was rigid. So rigid that it was clear he was doing everything in his power not to react. Why? Did he already know that the theater was in danger of going under? He had to. But that didn't explain why he wouldn't join in Ophelia's angst about the theater's future.

"Why did Curtis pull his funding?" I asked Ophelia, curious as to how she would answer. According to Patrick, it was because he was bankrupt. Did she know that?

"Your guess is as good as mine. I haven't the faintest clue. Curtis has been a steadfast supporter of community arts for as long as I've been at the helm of the Redwood Curtain Players. We counted on his donation year after year. It funded my salary and covered our marketing costs and overhead. Out of the blue, he told me that he was done. Just like that—poof." She clasped her fist and threw it open. "He gave no explanation. It makes no sense. His wife was a lover of community theater. She helped get the Redwood Curtain Players off the ground before she died. His annual gift was always in her honor. According to gossip, her deathbed wish was for him to use part of his inheritance to keep the theater running. She probably rose from the grave and scared the living daylights out of him—literally, last night when news started to spread that he was reneging on his promise. Can you imagine going against your dead wife's wishes?" she asked Jeff.

He drew a circle on the carpet with his foot. "No, that's rough."

Interesting. That explained Curtis's attachment to the theater. I hadn't understood why a guy like Curtis, who from all reports was known to be detached and a loner, had been dedicated to community arts. Knowing that his connection was because of his deceased wife gave me new empathy for him. It was also a reminder for me not to paint anyone with broad brushstrokes. Curtis was human, like the rest of us, and had flaws. But defining him solely on his flaws wasn't fair. He had left a lasting legacy of his love for his wife by supporting the Redwood Curtain Players. That was something to celebrate.

"He didn't tell you why he wasn't going to continue his gift?" I asked, taking careful notice of her facial expressions.

"No." She tossed a hand in the air. "He lumbered into my office, plopped on a chair, and said he had bad news that he wouldn't be giving me a check. I was counting on that money for the new year. We have enough in the bank to get through the next few months, but without Curtis's donation, next year is looking bleak."

Her face didn't betray her. I wasn't sure if that was due to her acting ability. If Ophelia didn't know that Curtis was bankrupt, it made her much less likely to have killed him, short of the revenge angle that Patrick had suggested. That sounded too far-fetched to me. The more likely scenario in my mind was that Ophelia had learned about Curtis's financial difficulties and had a contract that tethered his funds to the theater. If he were dead, whatever remaining money would go to the acting troupe. Of course, I had no idea if any such contract existed. And if it did, I needed proof.

"Did you and Curtis have any sort of legal agreement?" I asked, still examining her for any sign she might be lying.

She reached for the cigarette holder and tapped it on the edge of the coffee table. "It doesn't matter anymore, does it?"

"Unless he left us money in his will." Jeff spoke for the first time, appearing as stunned that the words spilled from his lips as Ophelia.

Her fingers slipped as she pounded the table, snapping the prop into two pieces. "Why would you say that? Don't go getting your hopes up for nothing. Curtis's money is gone. The sooner we accept that, the sooner we can pound the pavement to find a new donor." She scooped up the broken cigarette holder and her wig. "On that note, I'm due at an appointment. Do thank Hal for me. I'm glad to hear our performance was well-received, even if it is our swan song."

Jeff remained seated after Ophelia was gone.

"Is everything okay?" I asked, taking the spot she had vacated and resting the stack of kids' books on the table.

"Not really." He picked up a board book and flipped through it, like it was suddenly the most compelling piece of literature he'd ever read.

I scooted closer and leaned in, not wanting him to clam up. "Do you want to talk about it?"

"Uh, yeah, I guess." He blew his cheeks out and then sucked in the air. He ran his hands through his hair like he was trying to massage away a headache. "Ophelia is lying. Everyone's lying. And I can't take it any longer."

"Lying about what?" I kept my tone calm, wanting to create a safe space for him to feel comfortable to speak.

"Everything." He pounded the edge of the board book on his forehead.

That didn't give me much to go on. "Listen, Jeff, I know last night was stressful, and we're all still in shock, but if you know something that could be connected to Curtis's death, it's imperative that you share it."

He ran his finger along the words in the board book as if it were a textbook, and he was cramming for an exam. "I don't know. It's complicated."

"I'm here to listen, and if it's helpful," I said, trying to sound as open as possible. It was true; I wanted to hear what he had to say. "I can act as a liaison with Dr. Caldwell."

He looked up from the book. "You can? You mean if I tell you what I know, I won't have to talk to her again?"

"I can't promise that." I didn't want to give him false expectations. "But I can guide you. I studied under Dr. Caldwell." I added the last part in hopes that it would give him more trust in my abilities.

"Okay, yeah. I've got to tell someone what's going on. Otherwise I think I might have a full breakdown. Where should I start?"

"How about the beginning?"

EIGHTEEN

I had the sense that my conversation with Jeff wasn't going to be short, so I made myself comfortable in the chair. I wished I had my notebook or laptop with me, but he would probably be more at ease if I just listened anyway.

"How far back should I go?" Jeff asked, taking off his mangy coat and cap and leaning forward on his knees. His eyes traveled from the bookcases to the tea cart.

"The more information you can share, the better." I could tell he was uncomfortable. He couldn't sit still and wouldn't make eye contact with me.

He wadded up the cap in his hands and scrunched it into a tight ball—a telltale sign of nerves. I made a mental note but waited for him to continue.

"This isn't a secret, but I worked for Curtis throughout high school and college and until this last summer."

"Doing what?" I kept my tone neutral, but why hadn't he brought up their connection last night? That was a red flag.

"Anything he needed on the farm. He hired a bunch of students to do the heavy lifting for him. I worked in the orchard mainly, picking, pruning, and spreading manure in the fall—

that was not a fun job." He shuddered and made a gagging face. "I swear the overalls I wore still smell rank."

"Yuck." I didn't need him to expand any further on this topic. He'd painted a ripe picture for me.

"Yeah, that's what I did—grunt work. It wasn't pleasant, and Curtis was a real jerk to work for, but the money was decent and helped me pay for college."

"So you and Curtis go way back. How long have you known him?"

Jeff's eyes drifted to the tin ceiling and lingered there like he was studying the architecture of the period. "Probably ten years."

That explained their exchange at Penny's last night. They had a long history.

"He changed after his wife died." Jeff's left knee bounced as he continued. "He was gruff before, but after she died, he was angry all the time. He would yell at us to work faster and then complain that we were moving between trees too fast and missing fruit. You couldn't win with him."

This was all good backstory and matched what Ophelia had told us about the reason that Curtis was one of the theater's biggest benefactors.

"I'm a hard worker. I keep my head down, and I grind it out." He nodded his head with each sentence, trying to prove his point. "I just wanted to get the work done and get out. Some of my co-workers weren't as motivated. Curtis saw that, and he started giving me additional jobs. Nothing major—organizing equipment in the barn, that kind of thing."

"Was this early on when you were working for him?" I wondered again why none of this had come out earlier.

"Not at first, no." He shuffled his boots on the carpet. "He started me on basic tasks, like unloading fertilizer and seeds. When I came home during my first summer of college, he taught me how to use the backhoe and plow. I got extra hours.

He kind of put me in charge. Not officially, but I knew how to run everything, and I'd been there the longest. Don't get me wrong, he was no better to work for and I didn't get a raise, but it made the summer go by faster and I knew that I wasn't going to be a farmhand forever. I was studying acting, and once I graduated, I was moving to LA."

"Did you move to LA?"

"No, my mom got sick." His lips trembled. He gulped and rolled his shoulders back. "So I stayed in Redwood Grove to help care for her. It's just me and her. My dad left when I was a kid. I couldn't abandon her, not after everything she did over the years to put food on the table and care for me."

"I'm so sorry to hear that," I said with sincerity. Jeff postponing his dreams to care for his mom gave me more insight into his character, and given his emotional response to telling me about her illness, I was fairly sure he was being truthful, at least about that. "How is she doing now?"

"She's better now." He caught my eye and gave me a thumbs-up. "In fact, she's been encouraging me to make a go of it now. I've been looking at shared apartments in LA, but man, it's not cheap. I thought Redwood Grove was expensive, but we've got nothing on LA. I'm not sure I'm going to be able to afford to move."

I wanted to steer the conversation back to Curtis. If we got onto the topic of affordable housing in California, we might be here all day. "So you were basically Curtis's farm manager?"

"Yeah. He kept giving me more and more responsibility each summer, and then when I moved back in with my mom, he kept me on year-round. It wasn't great pay, but I've been able to save enough to at least cover rent for six months or more in LA."

I knew I had asked him to start at the beginning, but his story felt like it was meandering. "Going back to Ophelia and everyone lying, was this when you realized that?"

He scrunched the cap tighter. "Yeah. It happened one day

when the tractor broke down. I went to the barn to see if I could find a replacement part, and I found Curtis coming up out of a trap door in the middle of the floor."

"A trap door?" I let my mouth hang open. That sounded far-fetched. "For real?"

"Yes." Jeff nodded his head with force. "He was angry that I had caught him. He accused me of spying, which I wasn't, but then he had to bring me in on his secret. He made me swear that I would never tell anyone, and he threatened to fire me if I did."

"Wow. That's quite a twist; it's like something straight out of the pages of an Agatha novel." I motioned to the bookshelves.

"It gets better." Jeff became more animated. "Curtis was about to lose the farm. He had taken out a second and third mortgage and was in over his head. Rising costs paired with slip-ping sales did him in."

I kept my face passive but was glad to hear Jeff confirm what I had learned from Patrick.

"The farm was going into foreclosure, and a lot of people knew about it."

"A lot of people?" Patrick had implied the opposite—that no one was aware of Curtis's financial predicament.

"Yeah, this is where it gets kind of complicated. I've been stuck in the middle, and I don't know what to do about it. I didn't tell the police any of this last night because I'm worried that they're going to think I'm involved or have been covering up the truth."

"How so?"

His fingertips lost all color as he clutched the hat. "Ophelia flat-out lied to you a few minutes ago. She knows about the fore-closure. She's been working with Patrick to push it through. They have a master plan to take over the property together. He wants to develop the land, and she wants him to build a perma-nent community theater stage. I'm worried that I know too much and they're going to come after me. Ophelia can be, well... intense."

Patrick had warned me about Ophelia being unhinged last night. Was that to keep me off the trail of their partnership? "I understand how Ophelia would benefit from that partnership, but what does she bring to the table?"

"Curtis was already in default, and here's the kicker." Jeff paused and widened his eyes, like he was eager to share. "Ophelia used to work for the company that owns his mortgage. She still has friends at the company, and she's been pressuring them to push up the timeline. She and Patrick don't have a lot in common otherwise, but he promised that he would earmark funds to build a theater that she'll have complete ownership over in exchange for her assistance in making the foreclosure process go swiftly."

"Ah, that makes sense." I wondered who was telling the truth. Both Patrick and Ophelia stood to gain from Curtis's death. "Although I can't imagine Ophelia working for a bank."

Jeff laughed and loosened his grip on the hat. "Yeah, can't you picture her dancing around cubicles, noting numbers on spreadsheets while belting out a Broadway tune?"

"Now, that fits." I chuckled at the thought. I was so glad I had pushed Jeff to talk. This was a major breakthrough in the case. "You mentioned being in the middle."

The lightness in his eyes faded. "Yeah, well, Curtis knew what they were up to."

"He did?" I saw a flash of regret on his face. "Did you tell him?"

"No, I didn't need to." He shook his head and waved the idea off with his hand. "He already knew, and he had a plan in place to save the farm. That's what he was doing under the barn."

Now I was fully lost. Jeff's story was getting stranger by the minute.

"Curtis was convinced that the Wentworth fortune is hidden somewhere on his property." Jeff stared at me to watch my reaction. "There are underground tunnels and secret hiding spots all over the farm. Curtis had been meticulously searching them for years. You know the rumors about the Wentworth fortune, right? Anyone who grew up or has spent any length of time in Redwood Grove has heard the stories."

"Oh yeah, I'm familiar, but those are the stuff of lore and legend. It makes for good fiction, but it's not real."

"I thought so, too, until yesterday when Curtis pulled me aside while we were starting our warm-ups. He told me that he found a box containing money, gold, and the long-lost jewels in one of the tunnels. An hour later, he was dead."

NINETEEN

My jaw refused to shut. I couldn't sit still. I jumped to my feet and paced in front of the window. If what Jeff said was true about Curtis finding the Wentworth fortune, this changed everything. Were there actually tunnels under his property? Could that explain the wet footprints I'd seen in Penny's basement?

The questions came in rapid succession. Faster than I could process them.

Not a week went by when Redwood Grove didn't see at least one intrepid treasure hunter venturing through town and out in the surrounding farmland and trails in search of the lost cash. The historical society and museum had an entire display dedicated to the Wentworths' missing fortune. No one had ever been successful in tracking it down. Many people in town thought treasure hunting was a fool's errand. The more likely probability was the money and jewels were destroyed in the original fire or packed away in a trunk and taken with the family when they left Redwood Grove for good. Of course, that didn't stop savvy entrepreneurs from capitalizing on the marketing.

Every spring, the Chamber of Commerce hosted a treasure

run, complete with a map and chocolate gold coins for prizes. State of Mind Public House, a brewery and taproom, offered special menu items year-round: Pirates' Grog, a rum punch, and Treasure Chest Brew, a golden ale served with rock candy gems. Artifacts, the boutique on the village square, often rotated a few whimsical items into its eclectic displays, like picnic basket treasure chests, compasses, and vintage maps.

No one I knew actually believed the Wentworth treasure existed. It was a fun story and a way to connect our present to our past, but nothing more.

"Do you think Curtis was telling the truth?" I asked Jeff.

He shrugged. "I don't know why he would lie about it. He's been paying me to help him look for the money and jewels for the last few months."

"But he fired you?" I thought back to our conversation last night and what Fletcher told me about seeing Jeff applying for a job at Cryptic.

"No. He didn't fire me. I meant that I was out of a job because he was dead. He'd been paying me really well—all cash —under the table. Because the foreclosure was impending, he was on a tight timeline to find the Wentworth stash."

I wondered if Curtis would own whatever he found. That was a technical question for Dr. Caldwell, and I was not going to bring it up with Jeff.

"So you think Patrick and Ophelia realized that he found the fortune, and they conspired to kill him?"

"It's the only explanation that makes sense." Jeff nodded like he was trying to convince himself. "Curtis was talking to Trishelle. She'd been staying at the farm. I guess they go way back. She grew up in Redwood Grove, and their families were close. Apparently, Curtis's wife was like an aunt to her. Anyway, they were chatting before dinner, and I noticed Ophelia and Patrick eavesdropping on their conversation. As part of my role, I was supposed to pay attention to how guests were interacting in order to use that for improvisation after the fake murder. Patrick and Ophelia were up to something."

"Can you elaborate?" I paused in front of the tea cart and reached for a cinnamon spice cookie. "What do you mean by up to something?"

"It was like they were plotting together." Jeff scratched his cheek. "I don't know how to explain it other than I could tell that something was off with them. It made me nervous. I knew I was supposed to be in character, but I could almost tell that something bad was going to happen—then it did."

Could that explain why he'd spent the first half of dinner chewing on his coat collar? "Do you have any idea where Curtis found the Wentworth fortune and where it might be now?"

He shook his head. "No. He didn't say."

"Do you think it's still hidden in the tunnels? Could Ophelia and Patrick get to it?"

"They'd need a key to the secret hatch in the barn to get in. Curtis kept the key on him at all times because he was paranoid about losing it." He stuffed the crumpled hat in his pocket, glanced at the antique clock on the end table, and stood up. "Oh, shoot, I need to go. I'm taking my mom to a doctor's appointment this afternoon. I appreciate you listening."

"Anytime. I'm here if you ever need to talk," I said truthfully.

"I'm at a loss about what to do." His pained expression and wide eyes reminded me of a caged animal trying to break free. "I don't know what Ophelia and Patrick know. What if Curtis told them that I was helping him look for the money? Am I in danger?" He paced between the chairs, his voice cracking with concern.

"I've been trying to act casual and normal, but when Ophelia asked me three times this morning why I was being so weird, I started to freak out." The color drained from his face.

Suddenly he looked much younger and vulnerable. "I'm scared. What do you think I should do?"

"I think you need to get in touch with Dr. Caldwell immediately and share everything you've shared with me," I replied without hesitation.

"What if she doesn't believe me? It could look bad for me. I didn't say anything last night about the Wentworth fortune because I was worried that Ophelia might hear me. Now the police are going to think I intentionally withheld information from them. I'm in over my head." He ran his fingers through his hair like he needed to scrub away negative thoughts.

"I understand, but this information is vital, Jeff. What you've told me is going to change the direction of the investigation completely. Dr. Caldwell needs to know about Patrick and Ophelia working together to push the foreclosure through and what Curtis potentially found. Not only could uncovering the Wentworth fortune have implications for this case, it's of huge historical significance, too."

He tossed his coat over his shoulder. "Yeah. You're right." He nodded his head like he was trying to convince himself. "Yeah. I'll do it. I'll go to the police station as soon as I drop my mom off at her appointment."

After he left, I returned the books to the Dig Room. I already had plans to check in with Dr. Caldwell later. I'd give Jeff the benefit of the doubt and some time to follow through, but if he didn't tell her, I was going to fill her in on everything I'd learned.

"You've been occupied this morning," Fletcher noted when I went upstairs to our shared office to grab an advanced reader copy for a customer. His side of the room was plastered with movie posters, cover art from publishers, and his very own Sherlockian murder board.

I scanned my tidy bookshelves, which were organized by pub date and sub-genre. Thrillers and true crime were on the top shelf, followed by hard-boiled detective fiction, police procedurals, traditional mysteries, historicals, romantic suspense, and cozies. "You're never going to believe what Jeff told me."

"Try me, dear Watson." Fletcher did his best Sherlock impression by using a Sharpie as a pipe.

I stood on my tiptoes to reach a thriller that was releasing in two weeks. We were constantly inundated with galleys (also known as advanced reader copies). Publishers would send us early unedited versions of their forthcoming titles to garner excitement and in hopes we'd order large quantities for the store. Since there were only three of us, it was impossible to read everything that came our way. I'd suggested we offer ARCs to our most loyal customers in exchange for them sharing an honest review to be posted in the bookshop. Our "customer favorites" display had quickly become one of the most popular sections.

"Jeff and Curtis found secret tunnels under his house and farm. Not only that but Jeff believes that Curtis discovered the Wentworth fortune hidden under his barn." I waited for his reaction. This was right up Fletcher's alley.

He tapped the Sharpie cap to his lips, allowing a scheming smile to grow. "Annie, don't toy with me."

"I swear I heard it directly from his lips." I grabbed the book and placed my hand over the cover like I was pledging an oath.

"As Sherlock would say, 'When you have eliminated the impossible, whatever remains, however improbable, must be the truth.'"

"It seems believable. This area is known to have underground tunnels. Remember when we went on that walking tour in San Francisco?"

"Remember? How could I forget? I'm still convinced that Hal is holding out on us. There must be additional passageways here." He rapped on the wall to check if it was hollow. "His parting gift when he decides to retire is going to be telling us where they are. Mark my words, I'm calling it now."

"I would not be sad about that."

"What do you need to know about secret tunnels? I'm happy to give you a dissertation on the Gold Rush days when underground tunnels were used for drinking, dancing, and other vices. There are some dark pages in San Francisco's past. For instance, when the tunnels were used to coerce unsuspecting drunk sailors directly from the bars to ships waiting in the harbor. They'd then get sold to desperate ship captains. Obviously during Prohibition, they were used to smuggle liquor. All of that certainly must have found its way to Redwood Grove. We're only thirty miles away from the city, and the Wentworth family amassed their fortune in the shipping industry before landing here."

"That's very good to know and helpful. Thanks." I held the book. "I've got to get this to our customer, but let's keep thinking about how the tunnels might play into Curtis's murder."

He tipped his head and twisted his palm like he was offering up his knowledge on a platter. "Your wish is my command, Annie."

It was good to have Fletcher's expertise. He was a walking dictionary of Redwood Grove historical facts and lore.

I gave our customer the ARC and returned to my duties.

The store was relatively quiet for a Saturday. I figured it was likely due to the dramatic change in the weather. Couples and families strolled through the gardens, taking advantage of the late October sun. With it being the weekend before Halloween, plenty of other events and activities were happening around town. I enjoyed the leisurely rhythm of the day. It was a nice reprieve after last night. Fletcher's gothic mix played overhead while I rang up customers and answered phones.

Trishelle came into the store after lunch. I was surprised to see her. She didn't strike me as the bookish type, but she had mentioned that she remembered the store from childhood at dinner.

I was working at the cash register, packing online orders in book-themed wrapping paper. I looked up as she approached the till. "Welcome to the Secret Bookcase."

She looked different without her turban and floor-length party dress. Her style was California bohemian. She wore a pair of loose, flowing khaki pants and a peasant shirt layered with beaded necklaces and an oversized burnt orange sweater. "I had to swing by and see how the store has changed. It's been a long time."

"You mentioned last night that you grew up in Redwood Grove. Were you here for a long time?" I used my left finger to hold the wrapping paper in place while I tore off a piece of tape.

"Yes. Redwood Grove born and raised. I went all the way through kindergarten to high school and then took off as soon as I graduated." She appraised the Foyer as she spoke. "This doesn't look anything like I remember it. It used to be a dump."

"Hal's done a ton of work over the years," I replied, securing the tape in place and writing a thank-you note on the front of the wrapping. We gift-wrapped all our online orders and included little notes on the packages. It was just one of the ways to set ourselves apart from big-box stores.

"At least he's kept the character of the house intact. It's so disheartening to see so many of the old farmhouses and estates being torn down." She picked up a sweater weather candle and removed the lid to assess the fragrance. "I was glad to see that your friend Penny is also taking a thoughtful approach to reno- vations, especially with so much Wentworth history attached to the house. The Wentworth family are legendary. It's the first thing people ask me about when I tell them I'm from Redwood Grove."

"I agree. The eclectic nature of our community, including

the Redwood Grove folklore, is what makes this such a great place to live and I know Penny has been very intentional with every step of the renovations."

She closed her eyes briefly as she inhaled the scent. "It's funny how much has changed since I left and then how much is still the same."

"When did you leave?"

"Oh, a long time ago. I've been in SoCal most of my adult life." She put the lid on the candle and turned her attention to a collection of bookish socks.

"What brought you back to Redwood Grove?"

"Just passing through." She set down the socks and walked over to the counter. "I'll take this for sure, but don't ring me up yet. I'm sure I'll find more gems."

I set the candle next to the register for her. "Do you still have family in town?"

"No. My family is scattered." She sounded almost wistful.

"I heard that you and Curtis were close. I didn't realize that you knew him so well. I'm even more sorry for your loss."

She strolled over to the book display and ran her manicured nails along the spines. "Our families knew each other, but we haven't kept in touch."

"So you weren't here to visit him? I thought I heard you were staying at the farm." I didn't want to give Jeff up. I also wanted to keep her talking about her relationship with Curtis, but I was unsure how far I could push it before she would realize that I wasn't merely making casual conversation. She struck me as being astute and perhaps a bit untrusting.

"He offered to let me stay, but I didn't come specifically to visit him. It was nice of him to offer his guestroom in the farmhouse. I have so many memories from holidays and parties at the house."

I noticed she didn't elaborate on the reason for her visit. Was she intentionally keeping things vague? I was also curious about the true nature of her relationship with Curtis. Last night we'd all seen her walk up and slap him without any provocation.

"You seemed"—I searched for the right word—"frustrated with Curtis at dinner."

"Frustrated?" She deliberately raised one eyebrow and sighed in an annoyed huff. "What makes you say that?"

"Well, you slapped him." There was no point in dancing around the subject.

"Oh, that. It was nothing." She gave me a look that radiated superiority. "It was part of the fun. Everyone was supposed to be in character. I didn't hurt him. I barely brushed his skin with my palm. It was nothing more than a joke between old friends."

It didn't look like a joke last night. Curtis seemed stunned, and the smack was so loud that it made my cheek sting at the memory.

She tossed her hair over her shoulder. "It feels awful to stay at his house now that he's gone, so I've packed up my things and moved into a room at the Grand Hotel for the next few days."

"That's understandable. Was last night rough?" I reached for the next order to wrap.

"Rough?" She pulled a first-edition signed hardcover from the bookshelf and licked her index finger to turn the page.

I sucked my cheeks in to stop myself from screaming. Licking fingers was right up there with dog-earing pages for me. First-edition copies were rare, and collectors expected their books to be in pristine condition. Now wasn't the time to bring up the topic with Trishelle.

"It must have been difficult to sleep alone in the farmhouse knowing that Curtis was dead."

"Well, he wasn't dead in the house." She licked her finger again.

I cringed.

"I didn't sleep. Between you and me, Curtis shouldn't have been living alone. I'm shocked the house is still standing. The place is a disaster. Who knows when he cleaned last, maybe five years ago? I rarely sleep anyway, but I couldn't stop imagining bedbugs and other creepy insects crawling up my legs. I spent the night wandering through the... the house."

Was she going to say something else and stopped herself?

Everything about her body language came across to me as calculatedly casual.

"How long are you in town?" I tried another tactic, hoping I might be able to get more out of her if we weren't talking about Curtis.

"As long as it takes to finish some research I'm doing." She avoided making direct eye contact.

Ah-ha. There it was. "Are you researching Redwood Grove? The Wentworths? The whole town?"

Why the secrecy?

"In a roundabout way, the whole town, yes." She returned the book to the shelf. "I'm working on a genealogy project for my family. Tracing our roots. Everyone in my extended family grew up in Redwood Grove, but we're scattered now. It's going to be a holiday gift for my extended family."

"That's a lovely gift idea." I reached under the counter for a shipping box. Trishelle didn't strike me as the genealogy type.

"Yes, in fact, I should have you ring up the candle, and I'll take a few of these bookmarks and stickers, too," she said, approaching the desk. "I have a meeting shortly with one of the docents at the Wentworth Historical Society."

"No problem." I took her order and bagged her items.

"You and Penny are friends, aren't you?"

I nodded.

"Would you be a dear and let her know that I'd love to drop by in the next couple of days and take some photos of her property to include in my project?" Trishelle smiled broadly, flashing blindingly white teeth. "I don't want to intrude, what with the police and a crime scene on her hands, but if she happened to be willing to let me stop in to take pictures to share with my family, that would be wonderful."

"Sure." I handed her the bag and smiled.

She left with a small wave. I watched her until she turned down the gravel drive and was out of my sightline. I couldn't pinpoint what she was lying about, but I was sure she was withholding information from me. The question was, why? Was it connected to Curtis's murder? If they were old family friends, could she have had a long-running grudge against him? Or were they closer than she let on? What if Curtis had told her about finding the Wentworth fortune? Could that have given her a motive to kill him and keep the money for herself?

TWENTY

"Annie, why don't you call it a day?" Hal suggested as the afternoon wore on. "We're not busy, and I know you had a long night. You could do me a favor and drop the online shipments off at the post office, and then you can be done. Go home, put your feet up, watch some Jessica Fletcher."

"But it's only four." I motioned to the typewriter clock. I didn't want to ditch out of work early and leave Hal in a lurch, but I was desperate to get out to Penny's house and see if I could find a secret hatch or door in the basement.

"I believe it's what the kids call 'self-care' these days." Hal's bushy eyebrows reminded me of fuzzy caterpillars when he winked.

"You're so on trend," I teased. "Next, we should get you learning TikTok dances. You could go viral."

"Um, I believe the word you're looking for there is I would become a *meme*." Hal gave me an impish grin.

"Self-care and memes—Hal for the win." I lifted my hand to give him a high five.

"I'm quite serious, though, Annie. You've been through a lot, and I know you're highly skilled at putting on a brave face, but you don't need to do that with me. Last night was traumatic. It's okay to be gentle with yourself. Fletcher and I can cover the next couple of hours."

Tears welled in my eyes. Hal's kindness caught me off guard. Not that he wasn't always kind, but hearing his tender concern made me realize I should listen to his advice.

"Thanks, Hal." I brushed a tear away. "I guess I'm more emotional than I expected."

He came around the front counter to hug me. "That's because of your big, beautiful heart, dear Annie. We're all the better for it. You take care of us, now it's time to let us do the same."

I swallowed the lump in my throat and nodded, not trusting myself to speak.

"Go see Pri. Get an afternoon coffee. Maybe one of those Cryptic double-dark chocolate chip cookies and pamper yourself." Hal released me and kissed the top of my head. "Doctor's orders."

"I didn't realize you had a medical degree." I gave him a half wink.

"I'll have you know that I have a PhD in looking out for the people I love, and you're one of them, so you're stuck with my orders, like it or not."

"I love it." I blew him a kiss. "You're the best boss and doctor I know."

"Self-care, Annie," he called after me as I left with a stack of boxes.

On the short walk to the post office, I reflected on how lucky I was to have Hal in my life. It felt good to have him looking out for me, and I was going to take his advice, but first, I needed to make a slight detour—as in a beeline to Penny's property.

I hadn't been able to slow my heartbeat or cool the flush of adrenaline racing through my body ever since my conversation with Jeff. The thought of potential secret tunnels crisscrossing the vineyard and orchard was too compelling for my puzzle-loving brain to resist.

After depositing the packages at the post office, I crossed Cedar Avenue and headed for Cryptic, resisting the temptation to come up with an excuse to pop into the Stag Head. I could tell Liam what I'd learned from Fletcher, but I didn't want to look desperate or overeager, so I passed by and headed straight for the coffee shop instead.

The artisan coffeehouse was in a converted garage with large roll-up doors in the back that opened onto a patio. Purple and black garlands stretched across the front door. The twinkling amber and gold lights strung into the garland pulsed like little starbursts. Inside, the windows were steamy, and a "Monster Mash" mix played on the overhead speakers. A mixture of mid-century modern furniture and artwork blended in with the more industrial vibe of the coffee bar, exposed ceilings, and concrete floors. Succulents and miniature pumpkins were propped on the exposed wood beams where more garlands dangled from the ceiling.

Pri waved me over from behind the shiny espresso machine. "Hey, Annie, you're finally making an appearance. I've been waiting very impatiently all day."

"Sorry. We had a kids' event at the store earlier, and then the day just got away from me." I glanced around to make sure no one was listening. Customers were consumed with their own conversations on the teal blue and orange couches and collections of chairs throughout the space. The garage doors were open, but only a few people braved the patio despite the dry sky. This was California, after all, which meant anytime the temperature dipped below sixty, everyone broke out their Uggs and winter coats. "I did learn some pretty important pieces of information regarding Curtis's murder."

"Tell me," Pri pleaded, not bothering to ask me what I wanted before pulling espresso shots and steaming milk. "Penny's a mess. She went into the police station a while ago for more questioning, and I haven't heard from her since. Last night Dr. Caldwell was preoccupied with the basement. She asked Penny a ton of questions about who had access, how much construction had been done, and if anything had been done downstairs in the remodeling process."

I leaned over the counter and lowered my voice. "I think I know why."

"Hang on." She turned down the temp on the steaming wand. Then she whisked house-made syrup and spices into a ceramic mug, poured the shots, and covered them with the thick, hot milk.

I had no idea what she was making for me and I didn't care. Pri couldn't make a bad drink. I studied the specials on a small menu next to the pastry case. For Halloween, they were featuring a colorful lineup of drinks, including a purple ube dragon made with purple sweet potato, honey, oat milk, and espresso, a ghoulish green monster with matcha and cold brew, and a pumpkin cream latte with warming spices, pumpkin purée, and a splash of dark chocolate sauce.

Cryptic's aromatic brews and creative flavor combinations were one of the many reasons customers ventured from near and far for Pri's delectable drinks.

"Here." She handed me the coffee. "It's a mash-up—a chocolate spice mocha with orange zest and a splash of my house-made orange bitters. Let me know what you think."

I took a slow sip of the drink, savoring every layer. "It's like the most delicious thing I've ever put in my mouth."

"Don't say that, Annie." She smooshed her lips in a frown. "Give me constructive feedback to make it better, and then get to the good stuff. I want to hear what you learned. We have to help Penny. I think that Dr. Caldwell believes her, but if we can figure out who killed Curtis, then she'll officially be in the clear."

"I swear, this coffee is perfection." I raised my hand like I was pledging an oath.

"You're not a trustworthy taster. You never complain about any of my drinks."

"Because you're a rockstar when it comes to coffee." I raised my coffee and took another sip. "Now, do you want to debate your skills as a barista or talk through how we're going to solve this case?"

She tossed her hands up in surrender. "Murder, please."

I chuckled. Fortunately, there was no one waiting behind me, so I launched into everything I had learned from Fletcher and then told her about my conversations with Jeff and Trishelle.

When I finished, she bowed with her hands. "Why aren't you doing this as a career, Annie? I can't believe you got that much information in such a short amount of time. But the most important question is how did we not know there were secret tunnels under Curtis's property? And what if the Wentworth treasure has been here this entire time? Mind blown." She intentionally bulged her eyes out as she placed her hands by her temples and burst them open.

"I know, right?" I raised my vocal pitch and grabbed her hand. "Not just his property, Pri. Probably Penny's, too. The same goes for the money. The Wentworths owned her house so who knows what might be hiding in the walls or basement."

"What?" She leaned back and scrunched her face like she had heard me wrong. "You think there's a secret room or tunnel at Penny's house? Oh my God, can you even imagine?"

"My mind is buzzing like it's being swarmed by a thousand bees just at the idea." I drummed my fingers on the countertop. "Think about it. Where would the tunnel from Curtis's farm go? It's unlikely that it leads to nowhere. Tunnels were more common than people realize in the late 1800s and early 1900s when both houses would have been built. San Francisco has an entire underground network. Years ago, Fletcher and I went on a walking tour, and I remember our guide telling us about rumors of an entire catacomb of cellars in Nob Hill. Supposedly, the tunnels were built under the street between two homes on the hillside so the owner's mistress could shuttle back and forth without being seen. Secret tunnels and rooms were common again during prohibition, especially in vineyards. Wine makers needed places to stash their bootleg bottles."

"No way. And you think that Penny and Curtis's properties are connected underground?" Pri exhaled with a whistle.

"It would explain the wet footprints in the basement."

She gasped. "Oh my God, if you're right... I don't even have words. Why are we standing here talking about this, shouldn't we be in the car right now?"

"I'm all in. How soon are you done? Because there's one way to find out."

TWENTY-ONE

Luckily, Pri's shift ended by the time I finished my coffee. Even if it hadn't, I had a feeling she would have come up with an excuse to leave early. On the drive to Penny's, I texted Dr. Caldwell and gave her a brief recap of my day and to let her know what we were doing. Jeff should have had plenty of time to speak with her by now, and if he hadn't, then I couldn't trust him to follow through.

Sunset was at least an hour away. The sky was as clear as a cobalt sea except for a batch of puffy clouds skirting the base of the tree-covered hills in the distance. Weather often rolled in over the ridgeline. I wondered if the distant clouds were a sign that another storm was brewing.

Pri's phone buzzed as she navigated the two-lane road, swerving occasionally to avoid debris and downed tree limbs. "Can you check that?"

I grabbed her phone, plastered with coffee stickers, and held the door handle. "It's from Penny. She's running late. She'll be back as soon as she can, but it could be an hour or so."

"Crap. I should have texted her before we left, but my entire body is buzzing with the thought that the Wentworth fortune could be in her basement or somewhere nearby." Pri steered past a construction crew stringing new cable lines on the side of the two-lane road. "What are we going to do in the meantime? I don't have a key."

"Why don't we take a look around Curtis's property?" I suggested. Honestly, I wasn't upset that Penny wasn't home yet. Having extra time would give us a chance to see if we could spot anything unusual. I didn't think Jeff had fabricated his story, but it wouldn't hurt to see if we could find corroborating evidence of a secret space in the house or the barn. "Trishelle told me she's moved to the Grand Hotel, so his house should be empty."

"Ohhhh, devious, Annie. I like the way you think." Pri turned off the main road onto the long tree-lined driveway. Vibrant plum and apricot trees welcomed us as she slowly traversed the bumpy gravel road. The orchard appeared to be unending, extending continuously across the landscape. It was no wonder Patrick wanted the land. Curtis had to own acres and acres.

Pri parked in front of the old farmhouse. Its wood siding had been worn down by the passage of time and weather. Patches of peeling paint revealed the gray, rotting original wood beneath. Green roofs were trending in California, but I doubted the mossy patches and missing shingles on the sloped roof were intentional. Rows and rows of orchards fanned out as far as I could see behind the house.

"Damn, I can't believe Curtis has been living like this," Pri said, pointing to the second-story cracked windows. Many of them had been boarded up with plywood.

"I know, it's really sad." I noticed that even the porch swing had rusted. The impending foreclosure made much more sense now. I wasn't sure that the farmhouse was even salvageable. It looked like it might need to be condemned and completely torn down.

Aging boards creaked and sagged beneath us as we stepped onto the porch.

"You check this side; I'll check over here." Pri pointed to her right.

I peered into the bay window to our left. Inside was a parlor. I had to squint to see through the layers of grime and neglect. The furniture looked like it probably hadn't changed since the peak of the Wentworth family's reign over Redwood Grove. A fireplace with a hand-carved wooden mantel and brick chimney took up one side of the room. Bookshelves filled with yellowed newspapers, old magazines, and a collection of dated encyclopedias took up the remaining wall space.

A rounded doorway connected the parlor with a living room. I inched farther down the porch. The living room windows were eight-paned but flat, making them a bit easier to see through. Like the living room, the furniture was vintage but old, scuffed, and dusty. Nothing had been reclaimed or updated. It made me sad again for Curtis. It was as if the house was a time capsule, unloved and neglected for years.

"See anything?" I asked Pri, wondering if the house had been more vibrant when Curtis's wife was alive.

"Nope. Just the dining room, which looks like it hasn't been used in years—the table is piled with maps and newspapers."

"Same here."

I backed away from the window.

A crash thudded above us.

The swing sprang into motion, creaking on its rusty chains like an otherworldly apparition was controlling it. Another bang reverberated overhead.

"What the hell is that, Annie?" Pri ran closer to me.

"Someone must be inside." My heart pounded in quick, rapid beats. I looked above us, but all I could see were the cracked wooden slats of the porch's roofline. "Maybe it's Trishelle. She told me she was moving to the Grand Hotel because she didn't want to be alone out here, which I completely understand now. She could have come back to get her things."

"But there's no other car in the driveway." Pri pointed behind us with her thumb. "How would she have gotten out here?"

"True." I moved to the door and tried the handle.

"What are you doing?" Pri asked in a panicked whisper.

The handle turned with ease, and the door swung open. "We need to check it out. We're the only people on the scene."

"Annie, I don't know. This seems like a bad idea. We have no idea who's inside—what if it's the killer, and they're here to get the money?"

"We'll be careful, but there are two of us. It's still daylight. Text Penny to tell her where we are, and I'll do the same with Dr. Caldwell right now." I pulled my phone from my pocket and sent Dr. Caldwell another message before entering the house.

There was a musty smell in the entryway. Dust particles floated through the air. How long had it been since Curtis had cleaned anything?

"Okay, Annie, I love you, but this is the kind of thing that would have me screaming at the characters if I were watching a movie. What's the worst possible decision a character could make? This! This!" Pri pointed her fingers to the ground like flashing warning arrows.

I didn't want to make light of her concerns. "You're right, but we can't risk letting someone get away with the Wentworth fortune. Do you realize what it would mean for the town? People have literally been searching for the treasure for over a hundred years." My mouth went dry at the overwhelming thought of being the two people to discover the long-lost treasure.

Pri bounced on her toes. "I know, this is nuts. Absolutely bananas, Annie."

I agreed, but we also had to stay grounded in the here and now. The other pressing issue was Curtis's murder. "You're not wrong about the danger factor," I said. "I don't think it's very likely, but it is possible the killer could be inside trying to destroy evidence linking them to Curtis's murder. It's probably Trishelle, but let's say it's the killer, and right now, my money is on Ophelia and Patrick. I can't picture either of them having a weapon. Curtis's murder was pre-meditated and meticulously planned. I agree that we need to be careful, but I don't think we're in any direct danger. I also completely understand if you don't want to come investigate with me. You can wait here."

Pri laughed, breaking the tension. "Oh, right, and waiting here alone is the better choice? Seriously, how many times have we seen movies where we're yelling at characters not to go in the dilapidated barn or hang out alone? I'm sticking to you like glue, sister."

I squeezed her hand. "We've got this. There's safety in numbers. We're two kick-ass, modern women."

"Who are about to meet an untimely death," Pri said through a clenched jaw. She tilted her head to the side and stuck out her tongue.

I laughed and dragged her toward the stairs.

The staircase was a work of art with grand columns and an elegant hand-carved banister that matched the mantel I'd seen in the living room. In its heyday, the farmhouse must have been quite impressive with its curved doorways, stained-glass windows, and built-in bookcases. But I couldn't shake the feeling that Curtis had kept the house like a mausoleum. Maybe it was because the only light I could see was the sun filtering through the windows' cracks, casting hazy shadows on the floors and highlighting years of dust floating in the air.

Another thud sounded above us. Was whoever was up there moving furniture around?

"Come on," I said to Pri, taking stairs two at a time.

We reached the top of the stairs and stood at the landing to the second floor. "What do you think?" she asked, keeping her voice down and crouching behind me. "Should we announce that we're here?"

I gulped down a breath to stay quiet. "I don't know. Having the element of surprise on our side is probably a good thing, just in case."

She nodded and paused for a second. Her arms were at her sides in a state of readiness, like she was preparing for battle.

It definitely sounded like someone was dragging something heavy across the floor above us.

"There it is again," I whispered, noting the splotches of color spreading up Pri's neck and cheeks. "What are they doing?"

"Moving a dead body," she shot back with wide eyes as she bit down on her bottom lip.

"Let's be extra quiet from now on," I whispered, tiptoeing up the stairs toward the third floor.

As we reached the landing, I thought I was imagining things. A flash of white breezed past us.

My hands felt sweaty. A tingling sensation spread across my chest.

Was I seeing a ghost?

I don't believe in ghosts.

I blinked twice.

Was I starting to lose it?

The streak of white billowed closer.

I came to my senses.

It wasn't a ghost.

It was someone hiding under a sheet and they were coming directly at us.

TWENTY-TWO

"Duck," I yelled to Pri just as the ghost elbowed her in the stomach. She jerked back, nearly toppling over and falling down the stairs. I caught her as the figure darted past us and raced down the stairs.

This couldn't be happening.

Everything was wrong.

It was like a scene in a play.

A bad play, like the one I'd scripted for dinner last night.

"Are you okay?" I yanked her to the landing.

"No, I mean, yes, I guess technically, but that hurt." She massaged the side of her waist and clenched her jaw. "We can't just stand here. We have to go after them."

"Are you sure?" I checked her face to see if she was masking her pain.

"Positive." She nodded. "I'll probably have a bruise, but I'm fine. Really. Let's go before they get away."

"Fine, but stay behind me, okay?" I had clearly underestimated our assailant. I peered down the stairs. The ghost had vanished, which was impressive, since they couldn't be seeing well, given that their vision was blocked by the sheet.

Why the sheet?

Who was it, and what were they doing?

Nothing made sense.

I tried to ignore the voice of reason as we hurried down the staircase after the ghost.

We stopped on the second-floor landing. I figured the ghost would head down to the main floor and make a break for it outside. I glanced to my left and then to my right. To my surprise, I caught a glimpse of the ghost making a sharp turn down the hallway. The figure checked behind them and burst open what looked to be a bedroom door.

"They're boxing themselves in," I said to Pri. "Why would they do that?"

"Maybe it's a trap," she countered.

I hadn't thought of that. The only good thing was that when the ghost flew past us, I hadn't seen any evidence that they were wielding a weapon. Sure, there was a possibility that they had stashed their weapon in the room, but instinct told me that we had spooked them as much as they had startled us.

I approached the room with caution.

"Stay close," I whispered.

She dug her nails into my back. "Don't worry. I'm not going anywhere without you. As in nowhere."

I jiggled the handle.

The door turned easily.

"What do you say?" I asked Pri in a hushed tone. My heart beat erratically, unable to maintain any sense of rhythm.

"Uh, what do we have to lose, other than our lives?" She blinked rapidly, but pushed me forward. "Just do it."

I stepped inside. Like the rest of the house, the room had been unloved for years. A four-poster bed rested near a window. Yellowed sheets fluttered from the corners. The floor was coated in more dust. A dresser, couch, chair, and desk were all covered with the same faded sheets, but there was no sign of our ghost. The standout feature of the room was a wood-burning fireplace with an ornate grate. It was a shame that today's houses aren't constructed with fireplaces in every room. Sure, it was a necessity in the days before electricity, but there was something romantic about the thought of having my own personal fireplace. There was also something odd about the grate that I couldn't quite put my finger on.

My heartbeat thundered in my head. I could hear my heavy breathing and Pri's quick inhale. Otherwise, the room was eerily quiet. Too quiet for someone else to be hiding out.

Was the apparition we had seen hiding behind one of the other sheets?

That would be a smart move, blend in with the background.

"It's Annie Murray. I'm assisting Dr. Caldwell and we just want to talk," I said with more confidence than I felt. "Why don't you come on out, and we can get this sorted?"

Nothing.

Silence.

I turned to Pri. She shrugged.

I motioned to the couch. We shuffled toward it. I yanked the sheet off the top, sending tiny dust flakes in the air like confetti.

Nothing.

Our ghost wasn't hiding there.

I tried the desk next, the chair, and the dresser. Each time I pulled a sheet away, I stopped breathing in anticipation of having the ghost attack me, but they didn't materialize.

Now, I was more confused than ever. Our ghost had vanished in thin air.

"It doesn't make sense. There's no other way out," I said to Pri, trying to piece together how our ghost had made their escape.

"OMG, wait, Annie, that's it. This must be the room with a secret door or a secret panel. That's why they came in here. There must be a secret passageway out of this room."

I rocked on my heels and studied the room. "Where, though?"

Pri's eye followed mine. The walls on all four sides of the room appeared to be identical. Each had recessed wood paneling and wainscoting. The wall to my left had a large window that looked out to the sprawling grounds below us. Given the age of the house, there weren't any built-in closets but rather a large wardrobe.

"See anything?" she asked.

A fireplace with a once ornate wooden mantel was built into the wall next to the bed on the right. An iron grate had been shoved haphazardly into the bricks, but otherwise, like everything else in the house, the fireplace hadn't been used or loved in years. Thick layers of soot and ash made it impossible to tell what color the bricks had once been.

I shook my head. "You take that side. Try running your hand along it and see if you feel anything. There will probably be a switch, a latch, or maybe a part of the paneling that is more sunken."

The walls were coated in more dust. I coughed and waved my hand in front of my face to try and avoid breathing in the particles.

"How long do you think it's been since anyone's lived here?" Pri asked.

"At least a decade, but I don't know, with all this dust, a lot longer."

She coughed and brushed residue from her hands.

"That's it, Pri." I clapped twice and pointed at her like she was genius, which she was. "We don't need to run our hands over every square inch of wall space; we need to inspect the room for fingerprints. There is so much dust here that it should be easy to spot where the ghost vanished. Their fingerprints will be visible, right?"

"Way to go, Annie. Always outwitting me." She winked. "That's absolutely brilliant."

I shifted gears and turned on the flashlight app on my phone. "Let me shine some light over there." I went over to the far side of the bed.

Pri froze in place. "Shine it right here." Her finger narrowed in on the spot next to the bed.

Sure enough, fingerprint marks stood out on the dirty wall.

"That's it! We found it." Pri squealed, then quicky threw her hand over her mouth. "Should I press it?"

My heart rate sped up. I had no idea where the secret passageway would lead and if following it would put us in more danger, but my head nodded on its own like a puppeteer was controlling me.

Pri reached out and pressed her finger on the wall.

A screeching and groaning sound erupted as the panel beside the bed slid farther into the wall and then rotated to the side, revealing a dark, narrow passage.

"Holy crap, this is real." Pri's mouth hung open.

I was sure my face must have appeared equally dumbfounded. Things like this happen in movies, not in real life.

A damp odor wafted from the tight corridor. Unfortunately, it was too dark to see much.

"Hold up your flashlight again," Pri directed.

I positioned my phone so we could get a better look. Usually, I'm not prone to claustrophobia. However, that might change if we proceeded through the passageway. Cobwebs cluttered the low ceiling; none of it was Halloween decor. The wood used to build the secret escape route hadn't been milled smooth like the bedroom paneling. Splinters the size of my pinkie shot up through the floor.

"Uh, is this a bad idea?"

Pri nodded emphatically. "Yeah, it's a terrible idea. But I'm all in now. Let's go."

"Just be careful," I cautioned. Rusty nails and chunks of wood jutted out from the ceiling.

We made it to the end of the passage, which was more like a glorified closet.

"Um, okay, we have stairs." I came to an abrupt stop and pointed. "We are seriously in a secret passage with stairs; how bananas is this?"

"Pretty bananas," Pri agreed. "And to think you wanted me to wait on the porch and miss out on all of this."

"It's not too late. We can call it off now." This could be an ambush. Maybe our ghost was baiting us into the secret passage-way. They could be waiting to jump out at any minute and push us down the stairs or bash us over the head. After all they would have the element of surprise on their side.

"Never." She rolled her shoulders and breathed like she was trying to extinguish candles on a birthday cake.

The stairs felt like they might collapse at any minute. I took each step with caution as the boards beneath my feet sagged and bent from my weight.

Pri brushed cobwebs from her face. "I swear if I end up with a black widow bite from this, I'm going to be so pissed."

I laughed.

"What? You think spider bites are funny?" Pri sounded indignant.

"No, it's more that we're descending a *secret passage* on the trail of a ghost who could be a killer, and you're worried about a spider bite."

"For sure." Pri choked back a laugh. "Don't mess with black widows—those bites will kill you."

I tried not to think about the cramped space that smelled like a musty gym locker room. I knew it was probably just my overactive imagination, but it felt like bugs were crawling on the back of my neck as I tried to breathe through the thick, stale air.

Where had the ghost gone?

Did they know their way through these passages?

A vision of Jeff flashed through my head.

He admitted that he'd been helping Curtis search for the treasure. If anyone knew the house's secret nooks and crannies it had to be him.

I was semi-relieved by that thought.

Pri and I could take him in a fight.

We must have descended two stories because we finally ended up in the basement. The passage spilled into a large unfinished room with a dirt floor and a recessed window, which certainly wasn't up to modern building code. There was no way either of us could fit through the narrow pane.

I tried to take in our surroundings to get my mind off the replaying fear loop. The basement seemed to be a storage area. Crates, wine bottle cases, and vintage luggage chests were stacked on rickety shelving. A workstation in the center of the room housed tools that looked like they belonged in the Redwood Grove Museum. Dusty boxes of half-burned candles and antique stamps were bunched together with collections of tin coffee cans.

"Now what?"

"There's a door," Pri said, heading straight for the door.

"Wait." I stopped to grab a rusty hammer. "Weapon."

"Good thinking. Toss me one." She held out her hand.

I stuffed one hammer in my back pocket and gave one to her so I could keep the flashlight on.

"Now we can go head-to-head with this ghost and show them who's boss." Pri held her hammer over her shoulder in a show of power.

"Easy, let's not get ahead of ourselves. Think of these as a last resort—protection. We don't want to go on the offensive."

"Fine, but if that ghost comes after me again, I'm unleashing my inner barista rage on them." She twisted the door handle. It came off in her hand. "Crap." She tried to force it back in.

"Hang on; I've got this." I had taken a lock-picking seminar in college. I never thought I'd actually have a chance to put my lock-picking skills to the test. I bent over and wiggled the handle into its socket with small, gentle movements like I was playing a game of Operation that I had to win. Finally, finally, the handle clicked into place. In one easy motion, I turned it, and light from outside flooded into the basement.

It took a minute for my eyes to adjust to the light. Pri shielded her forehead with her hand. "How did it get so bright? I thought the sun was sinking."

I blinked hard. "I know—ouch."

After spots faded from my vision, I scanned the property. The secret passage had dumped us out on the opposite side of the house. Organic grapevines stretched behind us. The barn was behind us and the orchard to our right.

"We're in Penny's property, aren't we?" I asked, squinting towards Penny's house, which was less than fifty yards away.

"Yeah, but that means the ghost could be anywhere." Pri sounded dejected. "There are acres of grapevines, which stretch out into miles of untouched forest. We're never going to find them."

I agreed. It was a huge disappointment. But all was not lost. Finding the passage confirmed everything I had learned from Jeff. It also convinced me that Penny's and Curtis's houses were connected. There was much more to Curtis's murder than petty arguments or property disputes. We had stumbled onto something bigger and needed help from the authorities—now.

TWENTY-THREE

"What now?" Pri glanced at the grapefruit-colored skies. The sun was sinking, illuminating the vineyard. The sight was ambrosial. I wanted to stop to appreciate it, but we couldn't waste losing what little light remained.

I turned around and gestured to Curtis's house. "I want to go back in if you're up for it and take another look at the passageway. There has to be a second passage that connects to Penny's property."

"Have you heard from Dr. Caldwell yet?" Pri checked her phone. "Nothing from Penny. But it's only been twenty minutes. Why did it feel like we were in there for an hour?"

"I don't have a text from Dr. Caldwell yet either. Should we give it another look before it gets too dark?"

"Yeah. I mean, is every cell in my body screaming no at me?" She tilted her head to the side and grimaced. "Yes. Yes, it is, but of course, we have to go back."

We traipsed through the muddy grounds to the front of the house.

"Okay, let's take it slow and try to be methodical," I

instructed when we made it to the bedroom with the access door to the passageway.

"Right. I'll follow your lead." She waited for me to duck inside and then did the same.

The passageway was just as dark and narrow. Daylight made no difference. Not a sliver of light could penetrate through the walls enclosed in walls.

My throat narrowed. I tried to swallow but couldn't.

You've got to keep it together, Annie.

You're so close.

I inched forward, keeping my right hand against the wall. "I'm going to feel my way down. Just keep positioning the light on this side so I can see if anything jumps out, and so I don't trip."

My senses were on high alert as we began our slow and steady descent. The musty smell seemed more potent and more overpowering than it had a few minutes ago, but then again, maybe the anxiety was getting the best of me.

"Do you see anything?"

Pri shook her head. "Not yet, but my hands are going to be wrecked after this. I already have like a dozen splinters."

We spent what felt like an hour searching every square inch of the corridor for any sign of a latch or secret hatch with no luck. Finally, when we got to the basement, Pri sighed disappointedly.

"Well, that was a bust."

"Should we try the opposite side?"

"What choice do we have?"

"Are you sure you don't want to swap places? I feel bad that your hands are getting cut up while all I'm doing is holding a light."

"I'm good, I promise." She showed me her hands. "Just a forest's worth of splinters, no problem."

I chuckled, but the mood didn't feel light. This was serious.

We were potentially close to figuring out who had killed Curtis and where he had stashed the Wentworth fortune.

We didn't say much as we proceeded to the passageway's left half. After another fifteen minutes, we came up empty-handed again.

"I don't get it. It has to be here. What are we missing?" Pri asked at the top of the stairwell. "I've looked everywhere. I'm covered in cobwebs and dust." She tried to brush off her jeans, but it didn't do any good. She tapped her forehead with her wrist. "I wish my brain would start working. I feel like there's something obvious we're missing."

"Could it be in another bedroom or maybe the basement?"

"It's like everything is hidden within something hidden." Pri shook her head and twisted her lips into a frown.

"Hidden within something hidden." I repeated the phrase over and over again. "That's it. Hidden within something hidden. Take my phone. It's the fireplace grate. I noticed something was weird about it—look, it's all wonky, like someone shoved it back in at the wrong angle." I ran my hand along the edge of the doorframe until something clicked. "I've got it!" I pressed the recessed section of the frame. The fireplace grate swung open.

Pri yelped. "Oh, my God! You found it. You found it."

"I knew there was something weird about this fireplace. Remember how I mentioned that the grate seemed wrong?"

"Yes, you're a genius, Annie."

I took my phone from her and aimed it inside the fireplace. Tucked against the back of the chimney was an old, rusty metal box. "Do you think that's what I think it is?"

She pinched herself and then me.

"Ouch. What was that for?"

"I'm just trying to make sure this is real life. We've done it, Annie. We've done what hundreds of treasure hunters, historians, and experts haven't been about to do. We've actually done it. We've found the Wentworth fortune." She threw her hand over her mouth. "How many years has it been?"

"At least a hundred, no—even longer." I scooted to the side to make room for her. "You want to do the honors?"

"Sure." She crouched down and reached inside, looking at me with expectant eyes. "It's heavy. That's a good sign, right?"

"Right." I nodded in agreement.

Pri removed the box like it was a bomb about to explode. Her hands quivered as she set it on the floor before us. "Look at me. I can't open the lock. My hands are like Jell-O."

"I'll do it."

She slid the box closer to me and then reached out to squeeze my hand. "Whatever happens, Annie, there's no one else I would ever want to have an adventure like this with."

I smiled and gripped her fingers in solidarity. "Right back at you."

I studied the box. It was definitely old, bearing the marks and scratches of time. I wiped soot from the exterior wood, revealing a dark patina. The oak box had been crafted with exquisite care. Its sturdy frame was carved with motifs of the sea and native redwoods. The heavy iron was tarnished and worn.

I noticed something else—other fingerprints.

Had someone tried, unsuccessfully, to break into the box?

My hands were also unsteady as I jiggled the handle. Sweat pooled on my neck and dripped down my back. The treasure had been such a part of Redwood Grove culture and lore that it was nearly impossible to believe it was sitting in front of me.

I imagined opening the box and discovering rare gems—sapphires, emeralds, and diamonds. Would there be gold earrings and strings of pearls? Money dating back centuries? Heavy silver and gold coins minted before the invention of the automobile? Deeds to the property? Original schematics of the vineyard, orchard, even the city of Redwood Grove?

Whatever we found belonged in a museum.

Or would it be returned to any living Wentworth descendants?

Did any of the family members remain?

Had they all vanished after the fire?

Maybe the box contained clues to the mysterious disappearance of the family. Had they set fire to their estate and left Redwood Grove under the cloak of darkness? Or was it the more likely scenario—they had sadly perished in the massive fire that raged too fast and with too much fury for the local fire brigade to manage?

My body temperature rose as I pictured maps to territories that no longer existed and invaluable relics from the past.

I blew out a long breath. "You ready for this?"

"I'm ready." Pri bit her bottom lip, staring at me with her incredulous, shiny brown eyes. "I can't believe this is real. We're like the female version of Indiana Jones."

"I'm down with that as long as there's not a nefarious villain waiting to ambush us." My face split into a smile. I twisted the handle. The lock was tight. I tried again, this time wiggling it a bit to try and free it.

It worked. The lock clicked open just as a shadow appeared in the doorway.

I looked up and saw a gun pointed at us, just as someone yelled, "Don't move."

TWENTY-FOUR

My heart dropped. I yanked my hands away from the box like it had the potential to scald me.

"That's right, hands up, you two." Trishelle stepped into the room, pointing the gun at us. She was dressed in black from head to toe.

Had she planned to sneak off with the treasure once darkness set in?

"Back away from the box." She motioned with the gun. "Get up and keep your hands where I can see them."

I didn't like her piercing glare, which seemed to bore into me, or her caustic, cutting tone.

Her posture was aggressive like she was ready for an altercation.

"You? It was you?" Pri asked as we huddled together and got to our feet. I could feel heat radiating off her.

Sweat pooled on my neck. The walls felt like they were closing in on us.

Was it just me or was it hard to breathe?

"Don't put on the innocent act with me," Trishelle snarled.

"I know exactly what you two are up to, and it ends now." Her words were terse and lacked any hint of patience.

I tapped into every cellular memory of my criminology training. Trishelle needed to believe she was in control in a situation like this. Antagonizing her would only make things worse.

I kicked the box toward her with my foot. "Listen, there's no reason anyone else needs to get hurt. Take the box. You can have it."

"Yes, I'll take it." Every muscle in her body tightened. She clasped her other hand over the barrel of the gun to steady her arm. "I'll take it because it's rightfully mine. Curtis knew that and didn't care. He was trying to steal my inheritance right out from under me."

"Your inheritance?" I asked, taking a tiny step back toward the fireplace. "I don't understand."

"I told you not to move. Keep your hands up." Trishelle forcefully slammed one foot onto the floor, sending shock waves reverberating like a mini earthquake. She waved the gun at us again.

"I'm not moving," I said, cementing my hands in the air. "I'm just trying to understand why you killed him, that's all."

"You want to know why I killed him?" She laughed in a sarcastic tone that sent shivers down my spine. "Because he had to die. He deserved to die. He's been lying and hiding secrets for years. Secrets that tore my family apart. Did he care? No. He took great pleasure in making my life miserable. No longer. Those days are over. I'm taking back my power and what rightfully belongs to me."

My mind felt like sludge. I knew I should be trying to devise an escape plan, but it was like my brain cells weren't firing. Penny and Dr. Caldwell had both been informed about our whereabouts, and Penny should be arriving any minute—but would she arrive in time? How long had it been? Time was

198   ELLIE ALEXANDER

fuzzy, but I guessed an hour must have passed by now since we'd messaged. The light had faded outside, giving way to an ebony sky dotted with stars. Maybe it had been longer. I knew that in moments of heightened stress, like now, the body goes into "flight or fight mode," making the brain hyper-alert to process information at a rapid pace, allowing it to zero in on specific details to respond to the threat.

My brain was well aware that Trishelle was a threat.

She kept talking as if we weren't in the room. I recognized her dissociative behavior. That was a bad sign. Crisis intervention training had been part of my coursework. I knew that Trishelle was likely disorientated and potentially unaware of her surroundings. Extreme psychological distress made predicting what she might do next challenging.

"I did what had to be done." Her voice sounded manic. Her deeply flushed skin was an indication that her blood pressure was off the charts and quickly rising. "He needed to die. Curtis has been holding on to my family fortune for decades. The man had the audacity to tell me that the Wentworth fortune belonged to him. Is his last name Wentworth? No. I'm the rightful heir."

"Wait, you're a Wentworth?" I asked, stealing a quick glance at Pri to see if she was as shocked as me. I couldn't believe I had missed that connection. This was good, though. If we could keep her talking about her past and her family history, it would buy me time to figure out how we were going to make our escape.

"Yes, I'm a Wentworth, which means that the contents of this box belong to me." She sounded annoyed that I wasn't catching on quickly.

"I thought you and Curtis were old family friends." We had to keep her talking. And I was also worried about Pri. She had gone oddly silent. Her body trembled and convulsed in jerky movements. I couldn't have her going into shock now.

"That's one way of putting it. He stole my family's legacy years ago and I've been trying to find this ever since." She bent down to pick up the box, keeping the gun directed at our chests. "That's the entire reason for my visit.

"Okay, ladies, story time is over. Get into the passage." She motioned with the gun and paced from the bed to the fireplace. Was she trying to figure out her next move?

"What are you going to do to us?" I tried to catch Pri's eyes, but they were lasered to the floor.

"*I'm* not going to do anything to you," she replied in a sharp cackle. "I was never here. You two came searching for my family's fortune like any other treasure hunter and sadly ended up locked in the passageway you discovered. It's such a shame that a fire broke out and burned this place to the ground while you were stuck inside. That's how it works. History has a way of repeating itself. Some might call it the Wentworth curse." She made a ticking sound, like a timer counting down. "A shame indeed, but alas, there's nothing to be done."

I gulped. Was she going to burn the house down?

Pri didn't move.

"I said, get moving," Trishelle commanded. "I don't want to have to shoot you and drag your bodies in there, but if you don't get in there yourself, I will shoot you. Of course, they'll only find your charred remains, so a bullet hole isn't going to matter, but I'd rather not get my pants dirty."

"Come on." I held my hand out to Pri, dragging her away from Trishelle.

"What about your family fortune?" Pri spoke for the first time. Her voice sounded detached, like she was having an out-of-body experience, too.

"Sadly, that was never found either." Trishelle tried to make her voice syrupy sweet, but it just made her sound more sinister. "Could it have burned with the rest of the house? Possibly. Or maybe it was never here, to begin with. Who's to say?"

"We were so close, Annie," Pri whispered as the door slammed shut behind us. Her voice was weak and quivery like she was struggling to keep it together. "I don't want to die like this. What about Penny?"

The floor vibrated. It sounded like Trishelle was dragging furniture in front of the door to block the entrance.

"First of all, we're not going to die. I know it's scary, but we need to focus on getting out of here and then we'll deal with Trishelle and the treasure and everything else, okay?"

She bobbed her head in agreement. "Okay."

"Do you have cell reception?" I checked my phone. No bars.

Pri looked at hers. "Nope. You?"

I shook my head. "We've got to get downstairs quick."

"How long do you think it's going to take her to set the house on fire?"

"I have no idea, but I don't want to wait to find out."

"No, let's not stick around to see." Pri practically pushed me toward the stairs.

I took them three at a time, carefully keeping my balance while maintaining my pace. "How are you doing?" I called behind me.

"Better, thanks, but I'd rather be sipping a pumpkin spice cold brew in front of a crackling fire, to be honest."

I chuckled. It was good she was joking again.

The shock of being held at gunpoint had momentarily paralyzed her, but now that we were in charge of our own destiny, my spunky friend had returned.

We made it to the basement. I sprinted for the door that led out to the vineyard, but it didn't budge.

"Crap. She's locked it or barricaded it from the other side," I told Pri.

Tears welled in Pri's eyes and streaked down her cheeks. "Annie, I'm kind of starting to lose it."

"It's normal. Keep breathing. We're going to get out of here. I promise." I was fairly sure I sounded confident, but inside I was starting to panic. It felt like I wasn't getting enough oxygen. My chest clamped down, like it was lodged in a torniquet.

This was bad.

Really bad.

But I couldn't let Pri know I was struggling to stay in control and ignore the fear shooting through my system.

I wasn't sure what Trishelle was capable of, but I knew she was unstable and intent on getting away with the Wentworth fortune at any cost. At this point Pri and I were casualties of war she was willing to sacrifice.

I had to get us out of here. The question was how?

I didn't have time to formulate another question because a huge explosion shook the entire house and sent us both to the floor. Slats from the ceiling rained down on me. A ringing sound flooded my ears. I stuffed my fingers into them in hopes of making it stop. Was the floor moving, or was it my imagination?

Was I smelling smoke?

I tried to stand, but my knees buckled.

Debris littered the floor like confetti on New Year's Eve.

Had Trishelle planted explosives throughout the house? Is that what we'd caught her doing?

Had I made a fatal mistake by underestimating her?

The smell of smoke grew stronger as it wafted through the holes in the ceiling.

Don't panic.

Stay calm.

Think, Annie.

"Pri, how are you doing?" I extended my hand.

"Not good. Not good." Her grasp was clammy and damp.

I couldn't have her go into shock. Not until I found a way out.

"We're okay," I said, as much for my sake as for her. "We're going to get out of this. Just keep breathing."

Footsteps echoed overhead. It sounded like someone was running down the stairs. Had Trishelle set off the explosion too soon? Was she stuck, too? Or was this all part of her plan?

How many devices had she placed in the house?

The structure needed reinforcement without the threat of flames or an explosion. The farmhouse was in such bad repair that it wouldn't take much to collapse.

It probably would, and with us inside it.

I tried to stand again. This time I was successful.

"Can you stand with me?" I helped Pri to her feet, not telling her that my legs were quaking.

"I feel weird, Annie, like I might pass out." Her lids fluttered, her eyes rolling toward the back of her head exposing the whites.

"Wait here for one second." I headed for the window, hoping to let in fresh air and see if I could squeeze out of it.

It almost sounded like sirens in the distance, but I didn't trust my ears.

A door slammed above us.

Was it Trishelle?

There was nothing I could do. I felt helpless, and the smoke was getting thicker.

I could taste it in my mouth and feel it in my lungs.

Had one explosion been it, or did Trishelle have more damaging plans?

We had to find another way out of here.

One thing was for sure: It wasn't going to be through the basement. We would have to go back through the passage and see if we could get out that way.

The smoke was thinner inside the passageway. Could that mean the explosion occurred on the main floor or even downstairs?

I closed my eyes for a second in a last-ditch effort to calm my nerves and come up with a rational escape plan.

You don't have time to analyze the situation, Annie; you need to get out of here!

TWENTY-FIVE

I had to take control if we were going to get out alive.

"Stay here," I yelled to Pri, running to the passageway with newfound resolve. "I'll be right back. I'm going to find us a way out."

The house creaked like it was ready to cave in. I could picture the rotting beams bending and snapping like toothpicks. Every so often, a thud reverberated outside of the passageway. I couldn't be sure if it was just my imagination or if it was structural beams crashing from being weakened by the flames.

I huffed my way to the third floor. Pressure spread across my chest like I was being put in a chokehold. Maybe I had underestimated how much smoke had wafted into the interior.

It felt like I was breathing underwater.

My throat seared as if dozens of tiny needles were pricking it.

You've got to find a way out of here—now.

I tried the door handle on the off chance that Trishelle hadn't barricaded it.

She had.

It was solid.

I thrust my shoulder at the door and used my entire body weight to try and force it open.

It didn't work.

I tried again.

And again.

And again.

Sweat poured from my forehead. The claustrophobic space felt like the inside of a chimney. It was hot, humid, and even smokier.

My fingers blurred. My legs quivered.

Was the room spinning?

I gulped a huge breath of the smoky air and tried the door again.

It was pointless.

I went down to the first floor and searched frantically for an exit on this level. There was none, but my body was getting weary.

I stopped and closed my eyes. Suddenly, I felt very sleepy. My mind tried to convince me that I should sit down and take a rest. I knew it was a terrible idea and yet the urge was like a powerful drug.

Go back downstairs, Annie. You're going to have to try to fit through the window.

I slid down the stairs, letting my back rest against the bottom step.

If I just sit for a minute, I'll recharge and have enough energy to figure out plan C.

My legs slid down the wall.

Why am I so tired?

I just need to close my eyes. That will help.

I'll close my eyes for five minutes.

As I let my lids flutter shut, everything went black.

The next thing I knew, someone was shaking me.

Ouch, that hurts.

Not my shoulder.

"Stop, stop," I muttered. Or was I speaking? Maybe it was in my mind. Was I dreaming? Was I dead?

"Annie, can you hear me? Annie!"

"Huh?" I tried to open my eyes, but everything was fuzzy.

"Annie, open your eyes. You're okay." The voice was familiar and demanding.

I just wanted to go back to sleep.

"Annie, Annie, come on, open your eyes; I've got you." Someone shook my arm.

"Ow." I clutched my arm. "That hurts."

"Annie!" Liam's voice came through stronger as he continued to shake me gently. "Can you sit up?"

I clenched my eyes and opened them. The passageway was dimly lit by a single flashlight. I shielded my forehead and tried to focus on his face.

I must be dreaming.

Was Liam Donovan talking to me in a secret passageway?

That couldn't be right.

Nothing made logical sense.

I blinked twice and forced my eyes to open completely.

No, I wasn't imagining things. Liam Donovan was indeed crouched next to me gazing at me with such delicate concern that it nearly took my breath away.

"Wait, what's happening?"

Liam knelt next to me, clutching the flashlight under his arm. He sunk to the floor. "Are you okay? Are you having trouble breathing? Thank God, I found you. I've been worried sick. Penny's outside waiting for the paramedics, but I couldn't stand it. I couldn't just do nothing, not when I knew you were inside. You can't imagine where my mind went..." He trailed off and studied my face with sweet affection like he couldn't believe I was real.

I became aware of sirens and voices outside.

Was that water dripping from the ceiling?

"What happened?" I rubbed my head, which was a mistake. Pain shot down my right shoulder and arm like someone was twisting a knife into my bones.

"There was an explosion."

"Yeah... right." Why was everything so foggy?

"I'm going to lift you up, okay?" Liam stuffed the flashlight into the back pocket of his jeans. "We need to get you out of here."

"No. I'm okay. I think I can stand," I said, wiggling my toes and fingers to try and get blood circulating again. "I'm kind of shaky and out of it, but okay."

"Let's see if we can get you standing." He wrapped his arms around my waist to help me to my feet.

The pain was even more intense than before.

How had it gotten worse?

I puffed my cheeks out and closed my eyes.

"Your shoulder is in bad shape," he noted as he helped me to my feet. "Keep it pressed against your stomach. This might hurt, but I'm going to pick you up, okay? Hug your shoulder as close to your body as you can."

I nodded, not trusting myself to speak.

I knew I was dazed from the shock of the blast, but this was like a scene from a movie. Liam swooping in to rescue me and sweeping me off my feet. If everything didn't hurt so much, this would be an incredibly romantic moment.

"You ready, Murray?" Liam scooped me up like a rag doll. I let my body melt into his arms.

I winced as he lifted me.

"I'm sorry. I don't want to hurt you." He cradled me closer.

I could smell a mixture of soot, smoke, and ash mingling with his pine-scented cologne. "It's just my shoulder."

And my neck and spine and head, I thought.

It wasn't Liam's fault that my body felt like it was being stabbed by tiny shards of broken glass.

"Are you okay for me to take you upstairs?" His voice was soft and thick with emotion.

"Let's get it over with." I clutched his shirt and buried my face in his chest as he took the stairs two at a time.

I didn't want to look until we made it back upstairs.

I clung to him feeling a deeper sense of relief and protection than I'd maybe ever known.

Liam had me. He wasn't going to let me go.

"How are you doing?" he asked, ducking to get under the remains of the door frame leading into the bedroom where Trishelle had cornered us.

The bedroom looked like a bomb had gone off. Furniture had been tossed from in front of the passage door. Part of the ceiling had a giant hole. Chunks of plaster, wood debris, ash, and dust covered the floor.

The scene reminded me of Agatha Christie's descriptions of burned-out buildings in the Second World War.

"I can't believe the house is still standing," I gasped, taking it all in. My head still felt heavy and woozy. I was struggling to think straight. Everything felt sluggish and fuzzy like I was trying to swim through murky water. I was used to my brain cells firing at rapid speed, but they were currently moving slower than the gooey slugs on the redwood trails. "Did the explosion happen in here?"

"No, I think it went off across the hall." Liam shook his head, not releasing his grasp on me. "I'm not sure how much longer the house is going to hold, so let's get out of here."

TWENTY-SIX

Liam carried me carefully down to the first floor. I'd never been so grateful for his strong, steady grasp.

There was a flurry of dizzying activity on the main level. We squeezed past a team of firefighters dragging heavy hoses into the house. Lights from police cars, firetrucks, and an ambulance lit up the dark night sky.

Outside, more firefighters lined up in a single file row on the grass, dousing the roof with gushing streams of water. Police fanned out around the house, barricading the entrance.

"Is the fire out?" I asked, still trying to get my bearings.

Liam shook his head, paying attention to his footing as he stepped off the porch.

Someone was clapping and cheering.

I looked up to see Penny sprinting toward us.

"Annie, oh, whew. You're okay. I've been a mess waiting. This sucks, but thank God for Liam." She patted her chest twice in gratitude, but then her smile vanished. "Where's Pri? Where's Pri?"

Pri! Oh my goodness, Pri.

How had I forgotten Pri?

I pounded the side of my head with my fist, willing my brain to start working again.

Is Pri still inside?

I scanned the grounds.

A guy I didn't recognize, dressed in a paramedic uniform, jogged behind Penny. He reached into his bag for an oxygen mask. "Put this over your mouth," he commanded. "We're going to get you some extra air."

I couldn't have refused even if I wanted to, but my lungs burned, and my breath was coming in shallow gasps. Some extra air was probably a good idea, especially since my mind seemed to be processing at the speed of molasses.

"Let's put her over here." The paramedic directed Liam toward the ambulance where another paramedic was waiting with a gurney.

"I don't need that," I said, waving them off with one hand. "Where's Pri?"

"We're going to hook you up to an IV and run a few tests," the paramedic said, ignoring me.

"Is she going to be okay?" Penny asked, wringing her hands and glancing back and forth between the house and me.

The paramedic nodded. "Give her a few minutes."

"What about Pri? She was in the basement. Is she still inside?" I asked Liam through the mask. The momentary sense of relief disappeared. Panic soared through me.

Why wasn't anyone looking for Pri?

"Don't talk. The firefighters have entered the building. They're searching for anyone else still inside." The paramedic placed a blood pressure cuff over my arm. "We need to concentrate on you. Take some slow, long breaths. Your blood pressure is probably spiking."

I winced as he tightened the cuff. "Someone has to find my friend. She's in the basement."

"I'll go." Liam was already turning around and heading back toward the burning building.

Penny grabbed the back of his shirt. "Find her, Liam. Find her."

He nodded solemnly. "I will."

"Does that hurt?" The medic shifted position. He assessed my injuries before inflating the blood pressure cuff. "Let me get a reading here, and then we'll get you to the hospital."

I breathed through the tight mask while he checked my blood pressure. "I'm not leaving until they find my friend."

"The firefighters are searching the entire house for survivors. They're trained professionals. I'm sure they'll find your friend," he said, removing the cuff. "I'd like that number lower. But it's understandable given the ordeal you've been through."

"Do they know where to look?" Penny asked the paramedic, mirroring my concern, and then squeezed my hand. Her fingers were cold and clammy. "Liam will tell them, right? He knows to look in the basement."

I nodded, feeling a new wave of panic flush through my veins as the oxygen surged through my body. I wanted to tear off the mask and run back inside. I couldn't lose another friend.

Not Pri.

Not after Scarlet.

I refused to even entertain the thought. She had to be okay.

"Annie, I'm going to find one of the firefighters and make sure they're looking for her in the basement. I'm worried that Liam might have run inside himself. I'll feel better if someone else knows to look for her downstairs." Penny squeezed my hand tight and took off in a full sprint.

Feeling helpless isn't my strong suit, especially when my friend was in peril.

I tried to follow the paramedic's orders and breathe evenly, but until they found Pri there was no chance that my blood pressure was coming down naturally.

Memories of the day that Scarlet died flooded my mind—dropping to my knees when the police officers showed up at my apartment to break the news, walking through the quad in a daze, my cheeks ravaged with pockmarks and stinging sores from my unrelenting tears.

No. Not again.

Never again.

I firmed my lips together and shook my head just in time to see Penny and Pri walking toward me arm in arm with Liam tagging behind them.

"She's fine." Penny kissed Pri on the cheek.

Pri latched onto me and hugged me tight. "Annie, I was so worried."

"You were worried?" I sobbed through happy tears. "I'm a total wreck."

The paramedic checked her vitals once we finally pulled apart. She wiped tears from her eyes and wiggled her hands like she was shaking off the nightmare we'd just been through. "I'm okay. Annie took the brunt of the smoke."

I said a silent prayer of thanks to the universe while the paramedic continued to assess her.

"What about Trishelle? Where is she? Did you catch her?" I removed the mask so I could speak.

"Hey, take it easy. Keep the oxygen on," the paramedic insisted. "You're not out of the woods yet."

I tried to protest.

Liam put his hand on my leg. "Don't worry. Dr. Caldwell is looking for her now. She's not going to get far."

"The fire." I pointed toward the crumbling house, suddenly curious about how Liam had found us. "How did you know we were here? Because of the fire?"

"Yeah. It's pretty hard to miss. I tagged along with Penny to help finish putting her kitchen back in order and get my things —we got Pri's text so we figured we'd meet up with you both at her place. We saw the explosion as we were pulling into her driveway and raced over right away. The fire department is putting it out now," he answered. "They're also sweeping the property for any additional sign of explosives, so we want to get you out of here as quickly as possible, on the off chance that there could be more devices stashed inside." He turned to the paramedic. "Should we get her to the hospital?"

He took the mask off my face and placed an oxygen reader on my finger. "How are you feeling? Do you see spots?"

"No." I shook my head, answering truthfully.

A police officer approached the ambulance. "I have orders from Dr. Caldwell to take her to the hospital. She'll meet you there."

I hadn't seen Dr. Caldwell. Was she inside?

"Is it okay if I go with them?" Liam asked the paramedic.

The paramedic agreed.

"How long was I out?" I asked Liam, clutching my elbow to my body. "I didn't hear you until you were right next to me."

"We don't know for sure. Like I said, Penny and I saw the explosion. I've never driven that fast in my life. Penny called 911 while I tore out of the driveway and looped back around to Curtis's property. The ambulance and fire truck got here fast, but it took them a while to get the flames out and make sure it was safe before they could find you. I couldn't wait any longer. I'm probably going to hear about it from Dr. Caldwell and the fire chief, but I don't care." He paused, sounding breathless. "Don't ever do that again, Annie. I thought you were dead. I looked all over the first floor and couldn't find you anywhere. I never even considered that you could be upstairs. I thought there was too much damage."

"We found the passageway and the treasure," I explained, retracing our steps in my head. "Then Trishelle caught us. She had a gun. We didn't have any other options. Trust me, if there was another way out, I would have found it."

His eyes filled with concern. "My point is that you never should have gone in there alone to begin with."

"Yeah, that's fair. I didn't know what else to do. We were worried the killer would get away with evidence or the treasure. As it turns out, she got away with both." He was right, though. I had acted on impulse instead of following protocol. Dr. Caldwell wouldn't approve and it made me wonder about my career path. If I went to work for her, I couldn't make choices like this. I would have to follow the law to the letter. As a private investigator, I would have more leeway, but that was a thought for another day.

"It's going to be a bumpy ride," the paramedic said, shutting us in the back. "You're going to want to be strapped in."

Liam nodded. "I'll be right next to you the whole way."

I managed a smile as they secured my shoulder with athletic tape and got me into the back of the ambulance. "Hey, I have a question that's been bugging me," I said to Liam, narrowing my eyes.

"About the murder?"

"No. About your reading habits. There's a rumor circulating that you're deep into *The Hound of the Baskervilles*." I let the words linger, watching a coy smile tug at the corners of his chiseled cheeks.

"I have no idea what you're talking about, Murray. Are you delusional from drugs? What did the paramedic give you? Do you have a fever? Maybe you're hallucinating." He reached over and placed his palm on my forehead to check my temperature.

His touch sent an electric jolt through me. Suddenly, I did feel feverish, but only because of Liam Donovan.

I hoped he couldn't hear my pounding heart.

"So you don't want to join Fletcher's Sherlock book club next week?"

He shrugged and moved his hand away. "Never say never. I might grace the bookstore with my presence. Time will tell."

He was clearly taking great pleasure in remaining noncommittal.

I was happy to have our banter back and equally thrilled to be getting as far away from the burning building as possible.

As we drove off, my eyes lingered on what was left of Curtis's farmhouse. I couldn't believe Pri and I had been part of figuring out Curtis's killer and finding the Wentworth fortune. However, there were a couple of looming questions, like where was Trishelle now, and what had she done with the fortune?

TWENTY-SEVEN

Fortunately, the emergency room doctor confirmed that my injuries weren't that bad. My shoulder was banged up and bruised, but nothing was broken, and my lungs hadn't sustained any damage from the smoke inhalation. Pri also received a clean bill of health.

Dr. Caldwell didn't show up by the time they released us, so Liam suggested we go to the Stag Head for dinner and a drink.

"I think we could all use a reset and some comfort food," he said, keeping his eyes on me.

"Dinner sounds great," I agreed. I had no interest in lingering at the hospital, and I knew that Dr. Caldwell wouldn't mind taking our statements at the pub as long as she knew where to find us.

Pri laced her fingers through Penny's. "I'm all in for comfort food, and I'm so glad that we finally know who killed Curtis. I was so worried about you."

Penny kissed her forehead. "I was worried about *you*. We thought you two were dead. That could have been so much worse."

"Are you sure about my dinner offer?" Liam asked Pri,

giving her a playful nudge. "I thought you weren't speaking to me."

"Why weren't you speaking to him?" Penny asked, staring at Pri and then looking at Liam.

"Because he basically accused you of murder." Pri punched him softly in the shoulder. "I had to defend your honor."

"Defend my honor? What is this, 1718?" Penny threw her head back and laughed. It was a contagious laughter. All of us joined in. I didn't exactly understand why we were laughing, but it was the release I needed. My body felt lighter as we exited the hospital and strolled down the sidewalk toward the pub.

Evening ushered in a purplish tint to the sky. A swath of stars stretched across Oceanside Park. Halloween lanterns hanging from the lampposts glowed in a warm amber, lighting our pathway. The village was painted with colorful eggplant and marmalade twinkle lights. Storefronts beckoned us inside with their cozy displays.

This was the Redwood Grove I knew and loved.

I drank in the aromas of pizza grilling on the wood-fired oven at the Pizzeria and the briny hint of the sea lingering in the air.

My entire body sighed with contented relief. Sure, we hadn't heard confirmation that Trishelle had been arrested yet, but Pri was right. We knew who had killed Curtis and why. Dr. Caldwell and her capable team would surely be able to apprehend Trishelle and bring her to justice. It felt like all was right with the world again, or at least my little piece of the world. Which was more than I could ask for.

"You doing okay, Annie?" Liam casually wrapped one arm protectively around my shoulder.

"I'm better now," I admitted, leaning into him. "Although, what is the deal with you constantly riding in like my knight in shining armor? This isn't the Middle Ages, and I'm a highly capable, trained detective. I don't need saving. You realize that, right?"

"Would you ever let me forget that?" he teased. "And who said anything about saving you? You're the one constantly saving me."

"Ha! Exactly how am I doing that?"

"By being you." The tenderness in his voice made my heart quiver and wobble offbeat. "You don't get it, do you, Murray?"

My mouth went dry. I ran my tongue along the inside of my cheek. "Get what?"

"You're magical," he whispered in my ear, letting his lips linger for a minute.

The pulse of my heartbeat grew stronger, thudding against my chest like it was trying to escape. Liam Donovan thought I was magical?

"And you're maddening," he said as he pulled away, shifting into his gruff, grumpy old-man mode. "Do not ever scare me like that again, understood? That could have been so much worse."

This time, I couldn't blame him. "I agree. I wouldn't have gone back into the house if I had any idea that Trishelle had explosives or a gun. Once we realized it was her, I could tell that she was unhinged and ready to do anything to salvage the money, even if it meant burning down the house."

"Promise me you're not going to do that again?" he repeated.

"Promise." I made an X across my chest.

"You're falling behind us," Pri called over her shoulder. "Catch up because I'm suddenly so hungry I think I might order one of everything on the menu."

Liam chuckled and secured his arm tighter around my shoulder.

It felt good to have him next to me. Could this be our future? Could we be happy together despite our differences? The more time I spent with him, the more I was leaning toward yes. Liam had made a bad first impression, but every impression since had done nothing but thrill me.

He was a conundrum. A puzzle. A puzzle I wanted to crack.

At the pub, he pointed us to an empty booth and went to the bar to grab us drinks.

"You two are adorable together, Annie," Penny said with a knowing grin.

"Yeah, what's with the PDA?" Pri lifted her arm in an exaggerated motion and put it around Penny's shoulder. "Liam's got all the smooth moves."

"Stop. He was just consoling me after that harrowing experience."

"Oh my God, Annie," Pri practically shouted. "You're too much. Like we're going to believe that. Nice try, and if that's consoling, then please, console me." She made dewy eyes at Penny.

"It was a harrowing experience," Penny said, coming to my defense. "You were both in a burning building."

"True, but I fell apart. Annie was a rock. She kept me from completely melting down and went straight into the smoke and flames to try and get us out. I doubt that was harrowing for you, was it?" She shot me a challenging look.

"We're not here to debate and compare how we both reacted in a dangerous situation. The truth is I trained for scenarios like that, and as you know, I'm okay in the moment, I'm sure because of my degree and coursework. But trust me, when I get home tonight, I'll probably have a good freak-out."

Pri folded her arms across her chest. "Doubtful. You're unflappable. Unless Mr. Donovan is making his moves."

I couldn't hide the heat creeping up my cheeks. I was going to reach over the table and flick her with my napkin, but Penny did it for me.

She waved her napkin in the air. "I'm raising the white flag and calling a truce, but, Annie, I do want to sincerely thank you for your help. For a while there, I was beginning to wonder if I did accidentally kill Curtis. I couldn't figure out how someone poisoned him."

"Hey, speaking of that. What was the vial for? We found it in your entryway when we were looking for the key to the basement," Pri asked.

"The vial?" Penny looked confused.

"I'm guessing Trishelle stashed it there," I replied, having already been running through theories. "She must have known that there was a door in your basement that connected to Curtis's property. As one of the last living Wentworth descendants, she must have heard family lore and legend and she admitted to having spent hours and hours exploring the orchard, farm, and vineyards growing up."

"How did she do it, Detective Murray?" Liam appeared with a tray of hot spiced ciders, which he passed around before taking a seat.

"We'll have to wait and hope that Dr. Caldwell is able to get a confession out of her when and if she arrests Trishelle."

"Yeah, but you must have a theory," Pri said, taking one of the steaming drinks from Liam. "You always have a theory."

"I do," I admitted, feeling a blush on my cheeks deepening. "I don't think Trishelle accessed the basement on the night of the murder. I think Patrick was snooping downstairs. What I learned from Jeff was true—they were doing everything they could to get a hold of the property, and if Curtis found the Wentworth fortune, he would have had the means to save the farmhouse from going into foreclosure. I think that Patrick used the power outage as an opportunity to snoop around in the basement."

"Yeah, but we found the footprints before he took off." Pri used the cinnamon stick in her cider to swirl the drink.

"Right. I think those wet footprints belonged to Curtis. I

think he stashed the box with the jewels and money in your basement, Penny, because he realized that too many people, including Trishelle, knew that he'd found it. Trishelle would have inherited everything, so I'm guessing that Curtis was desperate to hide it somewhere safe. He must have done that before the dinner, but what he didn't realize is that Trishelle was watching his every move and knew every corner of this house. He didn't account for that."

"I'm still confused about how she physically did it." Pri sipped her cider.

Penny blew on her mug, letting puffs of steam circle in the air. "Me too. She wasn't seated near him at all."

"She didn't have to be seated near him. That's what the spider was for." I cradled my hands on the warm mug, thankful to be safe inside the Stag Head with its cheery wood paneling and scuffed floors. "She used it as a distraction. Everyone thought it was part of the performance, myself included, but it was a carefully crafted red herring. Ophelia said it out loud at the time. I just failed to make the connection. If you remember, she got up and poured herself a new glass of wine. She walked over to the buffet and polished off the bottle—that's why you had to get a new bottle in the kitchen. I believe she used that time to drop a few splashes of the vial into Curtis's drink. Then she slipped the vial into her turban. I thought it was odd how much she was touching and readjusting her headpiece. Now I realize that's because she had the vial of poison stashed inside it."

"You're way too good at this." Penny shook her head in disbelief.

"She needs to start her own private detective agency, doesn't she?" Pri asked, but it was a rhetorical question.

"Obviously." Penny raised her glass to me. "Okay, this is all making sense, but you mentioned that you found the vial of poison in the entryway. How did Trishelle get it there?"

"This stumped me for a while, too." I took a small sip of the cider. It hit the spot with tangy apples, earthy whisky, and aromatic cinnamon. "She probably ducked out of the dining room and hid it in the desk before the power went out. We were all busy chatting and going in and out of the kitchen. She easily could have slipped away for a few seconds without notice. I was hung up on Ophelia being stuck in the bathroom. I thought she was putting on an act because she'd been trying to get back to the entryway to retrieve the vial, but now I'm sure that was just an unfortunate accident."

"Faulty original hardware," Penny added.

"Yep. I can attest to that," Liam said.

"Trishelle snuck out to the entryway and took the vial while we were busy trying to free Ophelia. I'm sure she needed somewhere to stash it quickly once she realized the police were on their way. Otherwise she would have been caught red-handed."

Pri clapped three times. "Damn, Annie. We don't need Dr. Caldwell when we have you."

"I wouldn't go that far. These are just my working theories. Dr. Caldwell will be able to confirm whether or not I'm right."

"I'm confident that you are, and while we wait for the official word, I'd like to raise a toast, to my dear friend and our resident crime solver, Annie Murray."

We clinked our glasses together. The cider warmed my cheeks and the back of my throat. I was eager to hear what Dr. Caldwell had learned, but until then I was content to enjoy a fall cocktail with my friends, surrounded by people I cared about and the knowledge that we were all safe again.

TWENTY-EIGHT

We didn't have to wait long for Dr. Caldwell to arrive. She showed up just as our dinner was served.

"What terrible timing I have," she said with an apologetic smile, pulling a chair up to the end of the booth. "Please eat while your food is hot. I can fill you in on what we know at this point and wait to take your statements until after dinner."

"I can put in an order for you," Liam offered, handing her a menu.

Dr. Caldwell propped her glasses on her forehead and dismissed him. "That's very thoughtful, but I have miles of paperwork to complete when I'm finished here."

Pri tried to fit her hamburger in one hand. It was nearly as big as her head and loaded with bacon, a fried egg, heirloom tomatoes, lettuce, and house-made pickles. "Before I bite into this gooey, juicy beauty, my question is, did you find Trishelle?"

Dr. Caldwell gave us an assured nod. "We have made an arrest. Trishelle is currently at the police station, in custody, awaiting the arrival of her lawyer."

"Did she confess?" I asked, breaking the melted, cheesy crust on my shepherd's pie. The hearty meal sounded perfect for a cold fall night, especially after coming face to face with a killer and surviving a house explosion.

"Not to the murder, but we have evidence linking her to the crime, and I feel confident the DA will be able to build a solid case against her."

"What about the Wentworth fortune?" Penny asked. Like Pri, she ordered the burger with a vegan patty instead of meat. She cut her burger in half with a knife and took a dainty bite.

"We recovered the box, but I'm afraid it was empty. There was no trace of the famed fortune inside." Dr. Caldwell frowned and looked at each of us. "Trishelle claims it was empty when she opened it, but whether that's the truth is certainly up for debate."

"Do you think she stashed it or its contents somewhere?" I asked, scooping buttery mashed potatoes and the rich, meaty sauce onto my spoon. "And do you know if Trishelle would have inherited whatever treasure was found? Would it go to a museum? Or are there still other remaining Wentworth descendants?"

"I believe it's highly likely she found something. We apprehended her about five miles down the highway from Curtis's farmhouse. She was running through the fields. The problem is that there are acres and acres of orchards. She could have hidden it anywhere. My team will be doing a thorough sweep, but it will take a while to cover that much ground." She was introspective for a moment, studying the cardboard deer heads mounted to the wall. "As for whether or not she would have stood to inherit, that would be a question for the lawyers. I suspect there will be renewed interest in the Wentworth family in the days ahead."

"So once again, the Wentworth fortune is missing," I noted. "It vanished as quickly as it was found. It's almost like it's an enigma that doesn't want to be discovered."

"I would have to agree with that assessment." Dr. Caldwell

crossed her legs and leaned forward, resting her elbows on the edge of the table. "Any other questions I can answer? I know that you've all been integral in helping to bring Trishelle to justice, and I want to pass on my thanks and gratitude. Annie and Pri, I heard from the attending physician that you're both in good health, is this true?"

I nodded. "I'm fine."

Pri raised her finger while she finished a bite of her burger. "Me too, but I'll gladly press charges if that helps add to your case."

"Any news of the state of the farmhouse? Is it going to need to be torn down?" I took my first taste of the shepherd's pie. As expected, it was layered with flavor. The creaminess of the potatoes blended beautifully with the caramelized cheese and tangy tomato sauce.

"I haven't had a chance to speak in detail with the fire chief, but the initial reports sound like the structural damage to the roof and upper floors alone will require extensive repairs. Trishelle will be charged with arson in addition to murder."

"I still can't believe she's a Wentworth," I said through a mouthful of potatoes.

"She went to great lengths to disguise that fact," Dr. Caldwell said. "She uses her married name and tried to sever any obvious ties to her family legacy. Although it didn't take us long to trace her true identity."

"I don't understand why she stayed with Curtis," Penny said, voicing one of my questions. "Wouldn't she have been better off to fly under the radar? He must have realized fairly quickly what she was really up to."

"She needed to be able to search the property," Dr. Caldwell replied. "Otherwise, I think you're right, it would have made more sense for her to lay low, so to speak, but once she learned that the property was in foreclosure, it sped up her timeline. She had to find the money before the sale went through."

I scooped another bite onto my spoon, steam rising like a miniature volcano. "That reminds me. Ophelia, Jeff, and Patrick were telling the truth?"

"It appears that way. We have a digital thread of their email communication between the bank foreclosing on the property and other financial institutions involved in the sale. Ophelia used her relationship with her former co-workers to encourage the sale to go through quickly, but she didn't do anything illegal. Nor did Patrick. Everything with the foreclosure was standard protocol and on the up-and-up."

It was good to hear her confirm my theories.

"As for Jeff, he's been quite helpful and forthcoming. I intend to see if he'll assist my team once we begin searching the grounds and surrounding farms and orchards since he's very familiar with the area."

I couldn't think of any more questions. Dr. Caldwell lingered while we finished eating. Liam made her a cup of tea. She took each of our statements and promised to contact us with information regarding Trishelle's arraignment and trial.

"I hate to break up a lovely evening of almost getting killed," Pri said with a wicked grin. "But I'm so exhausted. I have to call it a night."

"What about cleanup?" Liam asked Penny. "Your kitchen is still a disaster."

"It can wait until tomorrow. That's my philosophy for life. There's nothing pressing about some dirty dishes." She held out her hand to Pri. "Especially after a day like this."

They left hand in hand.

"What about you, Annie? Nightcap?" Liam raised his eyebrows and gestured toward the bar. "I can make you a mean Irish cream coffee. Light on the coffee, heavy on the Irish cream."

A strong drink, or honestly anything, made by Liam sounded divine, but I was fighting to keep my eyes open.

"No, thanks for the offer, but I'm going to have to pass for tonight. I'm wiped, too. It's like everything has finally caught up with me." This case had prompted some deeper internal thoughts that I'd been putting off. I needed space to sit with them and think about what was next.

"Do you want me to walk you home?" He sounded hopeful.

I was very tempted by his offer. Things were different between us. I almost couldn't remember what it had been like to hate Liam. How could the man seated in front of me have irritated me so much?

Maybe because I hadn't let him in.

I hadn't given him a chance to show me his softer side. The Liam Donovan who was perfectly at home in the kitchen, who was reading *The Hound of the Baskervilles*, the Liam who had scooped me up in his arms and rescued me. I was eager to get to know him and let him see beyond the walls I'd built around my heart, too.

I was ready to take a risk.

I was ready to see where this thing between us might take us.

But tonight I needed to carve out time just for me.

"Actually, I think I'm good tonight. I'm going to take the long way through the park and let the healing ocean ions floating in the air work their magic. Plus, Professor Plum is probably waiting for me by the door, and you know you have some reading to finish. We have a book to discuss soon and I'm not telling you who did it." I pressed my finger to my lips.

"All right, but I'm going to hold you to a proper dinner date soon."

"Twist my arm." I offered him my arm.

He kissed the top of my hand.

I scurried out of the bar before he could see my reaction.

A quiet, calm walk through the park was just what I needed. I let my thoughts drift and merge, reviewing everything that had happened these past few days and reflecting on what might be ahead for me. A date with Liam, a meet-up with a source who might be able to provide me with insight into Scarlet's murder, and deciding once and for all what was the right next step for my career. It was a lot to process, but it didn't feel heavy or burdensome. Redwood Grove was home. I was content, happy, and strangely eager and ready to step into a new chapter.

A LETTER FROM THE AUTHOR

Huge thanks for reading *Death at the Dinner Party*! I hope you were hooked on Annie's journey as she continues to expand her bookish world in Redwood Grove. If you want to join other readers in hearing all about my new releases and bonus content, you can sign up for my newsletter!

www.stormpublishing.co/ellie-alexander

If you enjoyed this book and could spare a few moments to leave a review, I would be forever grateful. Even a short review can make all the difference in encouraging a reader to discover my books for the first time. Thank you so much!

This book was inspired by one of my favorite childhood mysteries—Clue. I spent hours playing the boardgame, trying to puzzle out whodunit and waiting with eager anticipation to tear open the manilla envelope for the final reveal. When the movie released in theaters, I was first in line for tickets with my bucket of popcorn and Junior Mints. I love the idea of Annie and Pri hosting their own version of Clue, complete with a raging storm and a power outage.

I hope the story inspires you to a host a murder mystery dinner and keep your guests guessing.

Thanks again for being part of this amazing journey with me and I hope you'll stay in touch—I have so many more stories and ideas to entertain you with!

KEEP IN TOUCH WITH THE AUTHOR

https://elliealexander.co

ACKNOWLEDGMENTS

Many, many thanks to Tish Bouvier, Lizzie Bailey, Kat Webb, Flo Cho, Jennifer Lewis, Lily Gill, and Courtny Bradley for your input, suggestions, feedback on Annie's world, and title brainstorms! It's so wonderful to have a group of readers and friends who are as invested in these stories and characters as I am.

To the team at Storm Publishing and my editor, Vicky Blunden, it continues to be a delight to work with you. I can't say enough about your professionalism, collaboration, and expertise! I'm so lucky to be in such great hands.

Nothing creative happens solo. I'm so grateful to my family and friends, who are always up for book adventures, research trips, and listening to endless questions about characters and potential plot twists. That means you, Dad, Melina, Heather, Garrison, all of my nieces, and a special shoutout to Gordy, Luke, and Liv for bearing the brunt of book conversations and always being up for more (or at least faking it well).

Made in United States
North Haven, CT
15 October 2024

58971456R00143